Laurie R. King is the *New York Times* bestselling author of 29 novels and collections that have won an alphabet of prizes, from Agatha to Wolfe. Books in the **Kate Martinelli Series** have been given the Edgar, Creasey, and Lambda awards, and were nominated for Edgar, Macavity, Anthony, and Orange awards. The **Mary Russell-Sherlock Holmes** stories include *The Beekeeper's Apprentice*, an ALA award winner and one of the IMBA's *20th Century's Best Crime Novels*. She is a third generation northern Californian who lives in the Monterey Bay area, and may be the only writer to have both an Edgar and an Honorary Doctorate in theology.

If you would like to find out about her future publications, sign up for the newsletter at:

LaurieRKing.com

BEGINNINGS

A Kate Martinelli novella
by
Laurie R. King

LaurieRKing.com

Ordering Information:
Orders by U.S. trade bookstores and wholesalers. Please contact Bookshop Santa Cruz Tel: (831) 423-0900; or visit www.bookshopsantacruz.com.

Printed in the United States of America

ISBN 978-1-73246-472-8

First Edition

14 13 12 11 10 / 10 9 8 7 6 5 4 3 2 1

BEGINNINGS

A Kate Martinelli novella

I

All stories begin. A newborn's wail, a doctor's news, the squeal of brakes on the road outside—with most stories, there's a place where you can look back and say, *That's where it started*. Where I met the guy, where I decided the life, where I took one turn and not the other.

And I heard once (probably from Lee, she tells me most of those things that stick in my brain) that a good story loops around, to tie up its end with its opening.

My name is Katarina Cecilia Martinelli. I've been a cop for thirty years, most of that time working homicide. My job is to build a story around a body—how it got there, who was responsible, and if it was murder. I know all about stories that are both an end and a beginning, because someone's end is where I generally come in, that awful chapter of a family's life that opens with an anonymous ring on their phone or doorbell.

I've done a lot of family notifications in my life, standing to deliver that devastating news. And not once, in all those years, have I said the necessary words without thinking about the night I was on the receiving end.

It was my second year of university, in the early weeks of 1983. Not a great time for me, and like a lot of college kids, I often buried my loneliness inside a boozy party. That's where I'd been that night, when I let myself into my Berkeley dorm room and stepped on a note someone had slid under the door.

Casey, see the RA, your family's trying to reach you.

Did I know? Standing there in my short skirt, big scarf, and illicitly tipsy brain, squinting at the sheet of paper in my hand—did I have any idea? I was twenty years old, troubled by a love I didn't yet recognize, alone while surrounded by friends, swamped under a load of classes for a major I wasn't sure about. The last thing I needed was for my family to reach out, to find out…

I remember a shiver of cold as I read the note—though if there's one thing I know from being a cop, it's that memories can't be trusted. And the days that followed, the weeks, were enough to scramble anyone's mental filing system.

I do know that I considered *not* going to see the Resident Assistant, *not* calling my family. It was late, I had an early lecture, and the last thing I wanted was to get sucked into one of my mother's problems. Into anything to do with Diamond Lake, for that matter.

But at twenty, I was still enough of a good Catholic girl to hunt through my change purse and walk down to the pay phone on the floor below. After all, it might be Patty who needed me. My kid sister, nearly seventeen, restless with hormones and stuck at home with The Neurotic.

Yes, it was about Patty.

And no, there was nothing I could do for her. Not any more.

II

Skip forward thirty-two years, after that winter's night of 1983. Yes, really—to the evening of March 24, 2015, when my wife and I were dressing for a party. And I was running late, as usual, because of work.

"Fifteen is not an easy age," Lee was saying.

"Jesus, fifteen. How can you and I have a fifteen-year-old daughter? Aren't you only, like, thirty?"

"Yeah, right. My dear thing, you and I both qualify for AARP membership. I'm ten years from Medicare. You are only three years from a full pension. We both—"

"Oh dear God in heaven, stop."

We were interrupted by a stern voice from downstairs. "Moms! We gotta *go!*"

I shouted back over my shoulder, half-buried in the depths of the closet. "Two minutes—I can't find my shoes."

"If it's the shiny black ones, I have them! Wear your other pair."

"Hey," I protested.

"You've had them for months and you never wear them. Come *on!*"

I crawled backwards onto my heels and glared at Lee. "When did our sweet baby turn into a teenager? She says she's wearing my shoes and I picture a four-year-old clumping around the house."

"She's nervous about The Boy. And speaking of ancient and tot-tery, could you hand me my cane? The pretty one."

"You okay?" She'd been sitting when I came in, so I hadn't seen her moving around yet.

"Fine, it's just the cold makes me stiffen up, I might need it later."

It wasn't the cold; it was the bullet she'd taken in her spine. Long years of grim therapy, cutting-edge medicine, and sheer luck meant that she walked now instead of using a wheelchair—but she would never stand up without considering how to do it. Just like I'd never shake the guilt I felt, every time I saw her brace herself to rise.

Because like I said, I'm a cop, with the San Francisco Police De-partment, and it was my very first case in Homicide that brought the gunman to our door. I did nothing wrong—nothing that every-one else in the department didn't do wrong, up to and including my then-partner, the great Al Hawkin. But it was Lee who paid for our collective inattention. The one who was still paying.

I watched her stand now. She was working to make it look non-chalant. At the same time, I could see it wasn't as bad as it some-times got in the cold, so I handed her the brightly patterned cane and headed downstairs.

I was distracted—by Lee, by the guilt, by dark thoughts. By the snark in a teenaged voice. And it was wintry, as it had been on that night in my dorm room thirty-two years before, and maybe there was something about the light in the hallway. Whatever the cause, when I looked down and saw Nora at the foot of the stairs, I blurted out something I'd never have said if I'd been paying attention.

"Jeez, you look like Patty."

She didn't normally—no reason she should, since they weren't biologically related. Nora's hair was blonde and curly like Lee's, she wore glasses, and she didn't always bother with makeup. Tonight, though, her hair was pulled smooth against her head, and she had on her new contact lenses. Also her makeup was pronounced and that salmon-pink she was wearing matched a shirt my sister had adored and that impatient tip of her head...

Anyway. Deep down in my traitorous brain, a long-buried mem-ory had twitched and made the jump onto my tongue.

Her frown deepened. "Who's Patty?"

Oh, crap. I continued on down the last stairs. "She was my younger sister."

"You have a—oh, yeah. Car accident, right?"

"Long time ago. Honey, you look fabulous. Even if you are stealing my shoes." I threw my arms around her—I'll admit, with a touch more emphasis than I might have, if I hadn't been trying to distract her. "God, you're a giant!"

The two inches of borrowed footwear along with the height she'd got from Lee meant that I—who'd come down the stairs barefoot, carrying the second-rank heels—almost fit under her chin.

"Just what every teenage girl wants to hear, that she's a giant," said Lee from behind me.

"Basketball players would," I protested.

"Oh, like I play basketball," Nora drawled. "Can we please just go? Logan's been there forever, and Daniel texted that he and Al and Jani just got off the freeway."

So I stepped into my shoes and fetched our coats, and out we went into the cold night air to Nora's birthday dinner, where friends were gathered and fun was had and nothing more was said about a long-dead aunt.

But this was Nora. Who, genes or not, had been born with a cop's inability to ignore a blatant clue. I wasn't surprised when the topic of Patricia Martinelli came back to life, the following evening as we were setting the table for dinner. Furious at myself, but not surprised.

"So," Nora said. "I Googled Aunt Patty."

My arm hesitated briefly in the act of reaching for the plates, but my voice gave nothing away. "You can't have found much."

"No, and it took me a long time to even dig up a little notice in the papers."

"I'm surprised there was anything at all. Single-car accident, not much to report. Can you grab the silverware?"

"The article said the coroners found no sign of alcohol or drugs."

"I think they decided in the end that she'd hit a patch of ice."

"Really? In California?"

"Well, it was winter. And the middle of the night."

"Had she been out partying?"

"She might have. Patty was… making some inappropriate friendships, around that time."

"Ooh, your sister liked the bad boys? But they did say she wasn't drunk or high."

"I'm not sure how thorough the lab work would have been, with no particular crime on hand. Hon, could you pour us some water?"

"Do you think she—"

"Nora, can we not talk about this over dinner?"

I knew the moment I said the words that it was a mistake, and indeed, dinner was punctuated by all the awkward silences and artificial small-talk a parent comes to know, and dread. When we'd cleared up, I had reports to write, Lee had a book, and Nora went to do her homework.

But later, while I was brushing my teeth, Lee said, "You know she's not going to let it go."

I spat and rinsed, pulled on the t-shirt and shorts I sleep in, and climbed into bed beside her with a book of my own. "Yeah, I know." I'd given Nora a clear signal that the death of my sister was both important and problematic. The kid wouldn't stop chewing at it just because I didn't want to go there.

"Why *is* your sister's death still such a tender spot, after all these years?" asked the therapist I married. "Is it because Nora's getting close to Patty's age?"

"I suppose. When I went off to college, Patty didn't have anyone to rein her back. She made some bad choices, then some worse ones."

"Nora hasn't made any bad choices." I looked at Lee over the top of my reading glasses, forcing her to add, "…to speak of."

We were both thinking of the same questionable choice: The Boy, whom we had sat across from in the restaurant the night before. And what kind of a name was *Logan*, anyway? Didn't parents think before saddling their kids with a Superhero's name?

Al, of course, had picked up my lack of enthusiasm over Nora's romantic choice. Al was her god-father. He'd been my partner for so long, we finished each other's sentences like a married couple—even now, five years after he'd "retired" to the SFPD Cold Case unit. He seemed to find The Boy's effect on me funny. So when he said in my ear as we were leaving, "Let me know if you want me to run his juvie record," I knew he was joking. Mostly. Though it was true, me being on active duty meant that a personal search could blow up in my face, while he had less to risk.

I thanked him, glared at The Boy to stifle any thought of a good-night kiss, and removed my fifteen-year-old daughter from the restaurant before things got ugly.

"Why couldn't she fall for someone like Daniel?" I grumbled to my wife.

"Daniel's twenty."

"I said *like*."

"She'll fall for someone dependable when she's ready to be serious."

"Hope you're right. What about you—did you ever have boyfriends?"

"I had friends who were boys, but no. I knew early on where I was going." Unlike some of us, who'd grown up wearing a shell of heterosexuality until the pressures cracked it wide open. "And Logan's not that bad, for a sixteen-year-old."

"Almost seventeen."

"Still sixteen," Lee said firmly.

"Good thing for him, or I'd have to go have a talk with him about statutory rape. The humiliation would make Nora hate me forever."

"I would pay to listen in on that talk."

"You'll just have to use your imagination."

"But seriously, Kate, you need to open that door and let Nora in. She wants to know about your sister. All you have to do it tell her why it hurts."

"Yeah, is that all," I muttered, and pointedly opened my book to read.

But the story in my mind when I finally turned out the light did not come from the pages. It came from my past.

My sister had died in a car wreck on a lonely central California road, two weeks before her seventeenth birthday. I'd seen her not long before, when I went home for the Christmas holidays, but we hadn't seemed to connect any more. That distance between us may explain why, for months after her funeral, my mind kept trying to shape her senseless death into a story—explaining her final days, hours, minutes. I never really managed to create a satisfying narrative. But as I lay listening to Lee's slow breathing, it came to me that my habit of visualizing a crime by fitting its pieces together—making a story out of victims and perpetrators, outside influences and time-lines—had started that winter with Patty's death.

∾

The car is traveling far too fast along Pipeline Road. The girl behind the wheel doesn't have a license—hasn't even passed driver's ed yet—but she "borrowed" a friend's car from a drunken party for a private joy-ride along the back roads of Diamond Lake. Freedom, daring, giving the finger to everyone who wants to keep her locked down out here in the sticks—mother, teachers, sister, friends. She races along, hair streaming in the wind, laughing at her own impetuous daring.

...No: no wind, not in January. The car would be closed up tight. But the grin on her face—the grin of the joyous troublemaker—that's there, for sure.

And of course, she's going too fast. And of course, she hasn't fastened any damn seat belt. The heavy old clunker shimmies a little on the uneven road, maybe finds a patch of ice, and when its inexperienced, slightly drunk driver tries to correct it, tries to hit the brakes, the wheel snaps around. She loses control and the car smashes into a tree.

Patricia Martinelli is dead the instant her skull meets the side of the car, with only a brief flash of terror to stain her joy.

III

There was nothing I wanted more than to forget it entirely, nothing I wished less than to open that particular door and show Nora what lay inside. But Lee was right. She generally is, when it comes to matters of the heart.

The next morning as I put Nora's toast in front of her, I said, "Let's talk about my sister after dinner. If that's good with you?"

She looked up, surprised and a bit wary. "Sure. I mean, if you're okay with it?"

I shrugged. "You're curious, which I get, but it'll take more than a five-minute conversation over the dishes. However, you have to finish your homework first."

She grimaced—but she did give me a hug as she was leaving for school. And I dutifully went to dig out the thirty-year-old shoe box from the upper reaches of the bedroom closet.

There isn't much left of Patty. After the funeral, when I was back in Berkeley, Mother had stripped my sister's bedroom and given everything away. Mother herself died only two years later, as if tormenting us had been all that kept her alive. And when I started clearing the house after that second funeral, I'd been shocked to discover that she'd stripped away a lot more than clothes and posters.

Every photograph of Patty was gone from the family albums.

9

My sister had been turned into a ghost of empty corner-mounts and blacked-out labels. At first, I thought Patty had taken them herself for some school project, or in a fit of adolescent rejection—until I came to the big, formal portrait from the family reunion when we were small. Patty and I had been in the front row. Only now, Patty's face was a neat oval of indelible black ink.

That was the day I burned my own past and buried its ashes, driving back to the Bay Area raw and naked and newly born. I had no past, nothing that did not fit into the two cardboard boxes in the trunk of the car. And in case you're wondering, no: being aware that my mother was mentally ill doesn't soften my dislike for her. She was an awful woman, manipulative and vindictive, even when she was being stable.

After my first shock of finding Patty gone from Mother's version of history, I'd launched into a furious and tear-soaked hunt through the envelope of negatives. Even those had been gone through—but after hours of squinting at the strips of film, I managed to salvage nine images of Patty that Mother had overlooked in her purge.

Those nine prints were in the shoe box now, along with seventeen of Patty's letters, a few bits of inexpensive jewelry that had survived because they happened to be in my room, and a caricature sketch of me in a cop uniform. (An oddly prescient gesture, since I never thought of entering the force when she was alive.)

Also, Thed Bear. A small, once-soft, once-brown stuffed toy that had been the focus of sisterly competition, one-upmanship, and barbed practical jokes throughout my childhood. Someone gave him to me as a birthday present when I was six or seven, and Patty had immediately claimed the bear as hers. I took it back, and thus a ritual began. I would notice that it was missing, and when I went looking, I'd find it in her bed and return it to mine. There it would stay, in with my other stuffed companions, for days or even weeks, until I'd happen to look around and discover it was gone again. As we grew older, the contest grew more complicated. I'd find Thed dressed in clothes from one of Patty's dolls and replace the dress with a necktie, arranging him on my desk or reading one of my books. The next time Patty appropriated Thed, she would mark her ownership by adding a bit of feminine jewelry—not removing what I'd given him, just overwriting it.

Gender was key. To me, the bear was masculine, and named Ted. (Not very creative, I admit.) To Patty, it was female and Theodora. Somewhere along the line, we'd compromised on Thed, but never compromised on our claim. And we never, ever brought Mother into the argument. We learned early that Mother's solution to conflict could be instantaneous and devastating, and neither of us wanted to see Thed thrown into the fireplace as other sources of arguments had been. Thed was private, Thed was ours, and Thed was a form of communication shared by no one else in the world.

Thed was scarcely recognizable as a bear, having lost some of its fur and much of its shape, while accumulating various holes, mends, ink, paint, and jewelry. Thed was fickle, siding with whichever sister had abducted him last, and changed sex with ease, moving from lacy pinafore to Roman toga without expressing a preference. Thed was a daredevil, having gone up in a neighbor boy's rocket once (and retaining the burn-marks). Later, he'd spent some weeks buried in the garden until Patty figured out my clues.

And very occasionally, Thed was a message of generosity and comfort, who would appear, unexpectedly, on the pillow of the sister in greatest need.

I'd never figured out why Thed survived Mother's scorched-earth final clearance of Patty's things. Was it because, sometime during my last Christmas home, I'd picked him up out of habit and put him in my room? Or had Patty felt my loneliness and agitation during that unwilling visit and, despite her own adolescent preoccupations, left him tucked under the covers of my bed?

It troubled me still, that I did not remember.

I touched a finger to the topmost necklace, a heart-shaped locket on a cheap chain wound around his neck, then closed the box. On the way through the bedroom, I paused to take down the only lingering presence of Patricia Martinelli in my daily life: a small watercolor painting of a flowering orchard that lived on the wall.

I carried the shoebox and painting downstairs, taking them to my office so Nora wouldn't spot them before she'd finished her homework. But as I did so, a thought worked its way to the surface.

Wasn't there some offensive image or idea in those letters? Something I shouldn't put into Nora's hands? I couldn't remember any specifics, just an impression strong enough to make me lift the lid and frown at the contents.

I pulled out the meager collection of snapshots, leafing through nine moments from my past. There was one of me when I was about eight, which would make Patty five. We were on a beach somewhere, arms around each other, laughing madly. Her dark brown hair gleamed in the sun, a strand blowing across her face. My grin had a gap between the front teeth. Happy girls on the sand, and I had no memory of the day at all. No idea who could have taken it in the first place, with Mother's camera.

Below the pictures lay Patty's letters, and my sense of distaste grew a fraction stronger. Something inappropriate in there? I ought to take them to work with me, to skim through over lunch, just to be sure.

I ended up reading the letters far more closely than I'd intended. They had been written roughly each month, beginning with my first week in Berkeley and ending a short time before she died. It felt like visiting an old friend on her deathbed, both painful and fond. Patty's words stirred up all kinds of memories that I hadn't thought about in years—things I was astonished to remember at all. A passing mention of smoking at school brought a vivid flash of the striped shadows under the bleachers. Her furious, obscenity-laced description of a school enemy who'd "accidentally" spilled her Coke all over Patty in the Village Bakery carried with it the jangle of a bell and the fragrance of baking yeast.

The next letter gloated over her revenge against the girl: detailed, subtle, and far more painful than the spilled drink had been, which ended up with Patty's enemy banned for a month from the bakery that was the social center of the town's high school students. As a cop and a mother, I was more than a little appalled; as an older sister, I was both proud and entertained.

And in her very last letter, sent in early January, I found the thing that had been nagging at me: a rude Polaroid folded inside a postscript page about a boyfriend, stuck in behind the main letter. As I read Patty's free-form scrawl, it occurred to me that the note—even without the accompanying picture—was designed to shock a staid and absent older sister. I became aware of a grudging smile on my face. Did I have any idea, when I was twenty, just how much of a mother I'd been to her?

All I remembered was the relief I felt, every time I ended a trip home and set off again to my Berkeley refuge.

The small collection of Patty memorabilia lay on the table when Nora and I sat down for our talk that night—along with a printout of the newspaper article she'd Googled, which I'd found when I went hunting. The one with the unnecessarily provocative headline that read, "Accident Puzzler".

Naturally, the first thing she saw was Thed, a formless brown blob nearly invisible beneath several garments, a dozen or more cheap necklaces over a crudely sewn neck-tie, and a plastic crown that didn't quite hide his pink mohawk haircut. His extremities all ended with tiny blobs of red nail polish.

"What is *that*?"

The weight of all those necklaces made it impossible to sit him upright on his own. I extricated him from the wedge of books and gave his disgusting fur an affectionate pat. Somewhere under several ounces of chains was a small unicorn I'd given Patty for a birthday present, the bear's first venture into the transsexual world.

"This is Thed. A very old and much-loved toy my sister and I shared."

Nora gave me a look and reached for the snapshots.

"That's your aunt Patty," I told her. "I put the dates on the back, as close as I could figure them out. And those are letters she wrote to me—which you're welcome to read, although they're mostly about people you don't know and bands you've never heard of."

"What's the painting got to do with her?"

"She did that."

"Really? Wow." Nora picked up Patty's watercolor, which had hung on our wall her whole life, and studied the flowering trees as if she'd never seen it before. "She was good. For a kid."

"I know. She could even do portraits, which are really tough."

"Why don't you have any of those?"

Damn. Why had I thought this was a good idea? Oh, that's right: *I* hadn't.

"Our mother burned them. Along with Patty's diaries, books, clothes. Everything, really, except what I had in my room."

Nora stared at me. "Why would she *do* that?"

"My mother…" My mother what? Was sick? Was evil? Was why, when Lee and I decided to have a baby, Lee had been the one to carry the fetus despite the risks of spinal complications? "…had problems. Mental problems."

"Really? I knew you didn't get along with her, but burning your daughter's clothes? That's just… weird."

"Like I say, she had issues. And I guess that's part of why I don't talk about Patty much. It hurts. Not just the loss of a sister, and not just the waste of a young life. It's… I was ashamed. I probably still am, to some degree. Because I got away, and Patty didn't. She would have left in another year or so, even if she didn't go to college, but when I went off to Berkeley, she was alone in the house with a… woman like our mother. Not that Mother was physically abusive, I don't mean that." No broken bones, at any rate. "Just, I suppose the word is *unrelenting*. When Mother was young, she'd wanted to be a nun, but her mother wouldn't let her. She ended up marrying my father instead, and had us. Then he died of cancer, not long after Patty was born, and after that, it always seemed like Mother blamed Patty and me for her unhappiness."

"That's just stupid."

I had to laugh. "I know. And if Patty hadn't been in that accident, she would have flown the coop and found her freedom, and my sister and I would be sitting here with gray hair, grossing out our kids with tales of our awful childhood."

My daughter looked down at the beach snapshot of the carefree sisters. "What do you think happened? In the accident, I mean?"

"Like I said, it could have been ice, or something ran across the road and she swerved to miss it. Probably a deer. It's a rural area, and she wasn't a very experienced driver—she'd only had her permit for a while." It never hurt to reinforce the dangers of driving, to someone who was already dreaming about her license.

"Wasn't she wearing her seat belt? They did have seat belts, then, right?"

"Of course," I said. "Well, maybe not the older cars."

"Was hers old?"

"Patty didn't own a car. Like I say, she didn't even have her license."

"Was it your Mom's car?"

"Good God, no. I would remember that." If Patty had ruined Mother's car, the complaints would still be ringing in my ears.

"Then whose was it?"

"Must have belonged to a friend. In which case it might well have been an ancient clunker with no seat belts and bad steering and brakes, since she'd started hanging out with the kind of kids she knew would drive Mother nuts."

Naturally, that led to questions about what Patty was like, and why she was getting into trouble, and so on. But although Nora was both a snarky teenager and innately curious, she remained at base a remarkably nice person. And because of that, she kept her questions shallow, to do with the what, when, and who rather than the more difficult matters of *why*.

Not that we were finished with questions regarding Patricia Martinelli. I knew the dynamics of my family well enough to see into the future: Nora would go away tonight, to all appearances fully satisfied. After a day or two, she would get Lee into a conversation and find out her other-mother's take on matters. Then she'd come back to me with follow-up questions and a theory of what had happened to my sister, and why, and very possibly, how.

Nora put the photos into the shoebox, clearly intending to study them for clues and revelations about me. When she hesitated over the letters, I suggested that she take them, too.

"Is that okay? I mean, they're private letters."

"No, there's nothing too shocking in them." Not now, at any rate. "And I think you'll enjoy them. She was a lot of fun."

"Okay." She added them to the box and put on its top.

"What, you don't want Thed Bear?" Nora shot the object such a dubious look that I had to laugh. "Yeah, he's a bit scruffy."

Before she went upstairs, she gave me a hug that was longer and more emphatic than usual. I looked at Thed, and decided he'd spent enough of his life in the back of a closet, so I propped him upright on a shelf in my office—where only I would have to look at him—and told myself that I'd handled things well. That it was good to get a family secret out of its crevice and into the air, and that now we could move on, our little family just that bit more bonded than it had been before my slip of the tongue.

And yet, as I lay there in the dark that night, under one roof with the two people I loved most in the world, a faint mental itch kept me from dropping off to sleep.

After Patty died, after my mother had followed her, I shoved my regrets and guilt and rage and everything to do with Diamond Lake into a closed safe, and did my best to forget the combination. One final trip of house-clearing and paperwork and bills, then I had turned my back on it all. Weeks would go by—months, even—without my thinking once of life before the age of twenty.

Now, however, with Thed on the shelf and the letters in Nora's hands, I could feel the first stirrings of relief. All these years later, mourning Patty might be a sadness instead of a punch to the gut, but it was nonetheless real. And now, it was out in the open. Maybe I'd begin at last to move on—in a good way, one that did not make me shy away from the memories. Okay, Nora was sure to have more questions. But I would answer her as best I could, without avoidance, even if she noticed the snide subtext of that little news article her Google search had turned up. If she did, I would deal with it. I would reassure her.

So why was I lying there with my eyes wide open?

It was that damned article. There would have been an earlier one that Nora and I had both missed, since this was clearly a week-later follow-up. And it wasn't so much the article itself as its headline that troubled me, suggesting things that weren't in the few lines of text. The headline was probably meant as a teaser, slapped on by some too-clever editor. If he'd led with something less coy—"Girl's Funeral" or "Lab Results from Crash" or something—would I be lying here, staring at the ceiling?

Instead, with "Accident Puzzler" followed by phrases like *does not appear to have been* and *usually* and *could indicate,* the piece damned by inferring what it could not openly say.

I was pretty certain that "Accident Puzzler" was going to be Nora's lead, too, when she came back to me. And it wouldn't help much to explain the business of selling local papers and headlines as eye-catchers, or to point out that car accidents happened, and people died, and there wasn't always an explanation for the idiotic calamities that fell out of the blue.

IV

I went looking for the earlier article the next day. As I had expected, there'd been one right after her death. I found it in the *Diamond Lake Clarion* on Saturday, January 22. The reporter gave her the full benefit of the doubt, less only the sad and foolish touch of not wearing her seat belt:

FATAL CRASH KILLS LOCAL GIRL

A seventeen year old girl died in an apparent one-car accident on Pipeline Road late last night. Police identified her as Patricia Martinelli, a student at Diamond Lake High School, and said that she apparently swerved to avoid something on the road and lost control of the car, going into a tree. She was alone in the car, and may not have been wearing a seat belt. Police are investigating the cause of the accident. Martinelli is survived by her mother and sister.

The later article, the one with the suggestive title that first Nora and then I had found, came out six days later. This one, factual on the surface, bore a very different message between its lines:

ACCIDENT PUZZLER

A one-car accident last Friday on Pipeline Road that killed a local girl does not appear to have been the result of alcohol or drugs, according to the Diamond Lake Police Department. "Usually when we see a single car go into a tree late at night, we look for intoxication, but it doesn't look like that is the case here. An examination of the site did show swerve marks, but that could indicate the driver was trying to avoid something on the road." A private funeral for Patricia Martinelli will be held tomorrow at St. Vincent's Church.

All weekend, the itch grew—the one that had kept me awake. All the time I was setting up for, staying awake during, and cleaning up after Nora's birthday sleepover of six noisy fifteen-year-olds with vigorous appetites, the itch was there. The same itch that chewed at me to find the missing elements of all the stories I built around my homicide cases.

It wasn't that I'd never turned my cop's mind to my sister's accident before. Several times over the years, I'd gone so far as to pick up the phone to see if I could track down her accident report in the storage vaults of Diamond Lake's police department. But I always set down the phone again, because I knew what that report would contain.

I've worked accident scenes. I've taken photographs, interviewed witnesses, compiled reports. Did I really want my memories of Patty overlaid by the brutal words and gruesome images of the last thing that happened to her? Have my fun, smart-mouthed, maddening sister turned into an object on a mortuary slab? I did not.

And yet...

When Nora came back, armed with the next set of questions, I wanted to be able to look her in the eye and say yes, I was absolutely satisfied that this was a sad but purely random accident. Surely it wouldn't take much time to clear away the nagging doubts introduced by that damnable, deliberately tantalizing headline? The only "puzzle" about the accident was why a small-town paper would bring a note of cruel uncertainty into its report.

You see, I'd grown up in Diamond Lake. I knew the language of its unspoken, understood gossip.

In that town—rural, conservative, and heavily Italian—sober driver plus Catholic funeral were code for suicide.

∽

Of course, if things had been busy, I might've let it go, at least for a while. But the weather was cool and clear enough to keep San Francisco's population from each other's throats, and I hadn't caught a new case in a while. That Monday there was nothing to keep me from picking up the phone and talking to the Diamond Lake Police Department about their accident records.

First, though, the computer. Were the roads icy? No: temperatures that night had been above freezing. And not even slick, since it hadn't rained for days. I had only a faint memory of Pipeline Road, but the maps I called up showed a three-mile long, dead-end road passing through farmland. In that area, there could have been anything from deer to dogs to a flock of wild turkeys that caused her to swerve.

I did have to wonder why she was there, since I couldn't see that Pipeline went anywhere. Maybe the dead-end wasn't as closed as the map showed? Could there have been some kind of private drive that, thirty years ago, made for a short-cut—the kind of road used by local kids who'd had a couple beers, trusting that no patrol car went down it?

(And yes, that is experience speaking. A lot of us cops weren't exactly lily-white innocents as teenagers.)

I shut down my browser, looked at the telephone, then turned instead to the paperwork I was paid to do. But either the world had a message for me, or my eyes were attuned to anything related to Patty's death, because there on my desk was a printout with a list of witnesses in need of interviewing. One address was a town in San Joaquin County. A town I knew was maybe a dozen miles from Diamond Lake.

These were not my witnesses. It wasn't my case. No reason to volunteer... but I did. And considering the boring drive, freeways into farmland, my offer was quickly snatched up. I called the number for the witness. Would this afternoon be convenient?

Some things only get done if you don't stop to think about them.

Two hours later, I was driving past a thing I hadn't laid eyes on in more than twenty years. The sign that read:

WELCOME TO DIAMOND LAKE
A FRIENDLY COMMUNITY

It was not the same sign that used to make my stomach clench when I'd spot it through the Greyhound bus window. This one was new, wide, and looked as if it had cost the town a chunk of money. The well-maintained flower bed around its base showed patches of spring color.

The Diamond Lake I knew was one of those farming communities left high and dry when the interstate was laid, inconvenient for travelers needing to fill their tanks and their stomachs. It would not have surprised me if you'd told me back then that, at the age of 52, I'd find nothing here but tumbleweeds and a sign obscured by rust and bullet holes.

The next surprise was the dull, dingy high school I'd endured for four long years, now polished and planted, its street-front offices dwarfed by a huge new building rising behind. Nearing the school entrance road, I slowed to read the letters on the side, ten feet high and no doubt visible from every upper story in town.

MARK FIELDS HALL

The school and its giant hall on top of the cheerful sign at the town entrance all hit me at once, as if I'd been ambushed by a stranger in my living room. My pulse rose, my grip on the wheel went tight under the threat of adolescent tortures and non-belonging, the thoughts of a girl who would grow up lesbian but who at the time—

A motion alarmingly close to the front of the car had my foot slamming onto the brake, and another dose of adrenaline flooded in.

The kid had been about to step into the marked and lighted

crosswalk. He glared at my fender, a bare six feet from his leg, then at me. I lifted my hands in apology. He shook his head in disgust before stepping down from the curb. "Sorry!" I called. I wasn't surprised when his reply was a jab of the middle finger.

I'd killed the engine. Taking a deep breath, I started it again, got the car into gear, and went on, paying attention to what was actually going on outside my windows.

The high school was planted with trees and lawns so green they looked artificial, wrapped around parking lots filled with shiny cars. At the end of the school grounds, a series of eager franchises like Starbucks and McDonald's made it clear that as soon as the noon bell rang, the area would be a sea of students with money.

Half a mile of familiar logos finally gave way to the strip-mall businesses run by locals: manicure and hair salons, chiropractors and dentists. After those came the town itself, with shapes that I remembered—movie theater, public library, looming red brick Catholic church, and two blocks of stores linked by a Western-style covered sidewalk. Here, too, the colors seemed unnaturally bright, the Fifties outlines less old-fashioned and more deliberately retro.

I saw several new buildings, and very few For Rent signs. The stores and restaurants looked mid-range rather than upscale, with only one obvious art gallery, but the street parking in front of them held nearly as many hybrid cars as pickup trucks. And when I noticed three men in dark suits walking into one of the new office buildings, they didn't look like something the aliens had dropped off.

Diamond Lake had gone prosperous.

I was so distracted by the strange familiar town that the woman behind me—a BMW, no less—laid on her horn in annoyance. I pulled into a loading-only space, giving her an apologetic wave, and turned off the engine. Why the hell was I driving like a birdbrain?

The answer was not hard to find. Because I hated this place. Because I had worked very hard to leave it behind, to forget everything it had tried to teach me. This "Friendly Community" had made a policy out of overlooking bruised faces and wounded spirits. This community had killed my sister. I might have volunteered to come here, but I was doing it for Nora, and had no intention of offering the place any forgiveness.

I set the phone's map function with the address for my potential witness, some ten miles further on, and got back on the road.

The woman turned out to be as unexpected as the rest of Diamond Lake, a cheerful Somali web designer recently elected to the city council. Thirty years ago, she'd have collected gawkers every time she walked down Main Street.

To my even greater pleasure, her statement did actually provide some solid information. In less than an hour, I was handing her my card, shaking her hand, and giving her the thanks of the SFPD.

Marginally cheered by this justification of taxpayer money and departmental time, I re-set my phone for Pipeline Road.

Going there now was pointless, I knew. Not only did I have no idea where Patty's accident had taken place, but even if I did, there'd be no trace left. Still, I wanted at least to see it, and found it coming into the main road a couple miles south of town.

Pipeline had obviously started as a dirt track between fields. At some point it had been paved, with drainage ditches between its asphalt surface and the adjoining fields—half-green winter hay on one side, walnut orchard on the other. Potholes had begun to take over, leaving portions of its two-lane width largely theoretical. The road went straight, with the occasional curve around a field or some feature too heavy for a plow to ignore. Much of it was bordered by huge eucalyptus trees, put in by some early settler to block the wind or suck up a swampy patch. Narrow gaps in their ranks had been used for access lanes to the orchard and the hay field, with rusty metal gates nearly overgrown by weeds and blackberry vines.

I remembered those trees. Which meant I'd been along here, back in the Dark Ages.

The road ended in a fence topped with rusty barbed wire and No Trespassing signs. Through the gate lay a sprawl of derelict, graffiti-stained industrial buildings, whose faded sign declared it Johnson's Quarry. Its padlocked gates explained both the once-good road and the present lack of traffic: this wasn't a short cut to anywhere.

Driving back down Pipeline toward town, I eyed the huge old trees, but there was no way of knowing which of their scars and bashes had been a part of my sister's death. If any.

When I reached the town again, I nearly kept going, back to the freeway and home. Even when Diamond Lake had worn a familiar face, there was no welcome here. If I'd had a different mother? Maybe. All I knew was that I wanted to go home.

And yet: Nora was going to have questions.

When my foot decided at last to move to the brakes, I was already past the sign for the Diamond Lake Police Department. But there was parking along the street, so I pulled into a spot, pushed a few coins into the meter, and walked back.

The DLPD was another new building, facing the town park—which had a working fountain, a luxury in drought country. The building was fronted with nothing-to-hide-here windows of bulletproof glass and flower-filled planters massive enough to repel a tank. Inside, there were paintings by a local artist instead of wanted posters, industrial carpet instead of worn lino, and bright cushioned seats in place of worn benches. One corner had a collection of kids' toys, some of which were hardly broken.

It came as something of a relief to find that all this welcoming outreach stopped with the man on the desk who, though young, was as stolid and unhelpful as any grizzled veteran of a thousand Saturday nights.

I explained, in simple words, who I was and what I was hoping to find. He appeared to listen, but it was only an appearance.

"There was a homicide on Pipeline Road?"

"No, sorry. *I'm* with Homicide—SFPD. San Francisco. That's what I do. This concerns an *accident*, thirty years ago, that I'd like some information on. A car crash."

"You're investigating a car crash?"

"No, it's got nothing to do with an investigation, I'd just like—"

Fortunately for both my blood pressure and his neck, we were interrupted by a voice from a propped-open fire door, probably left that way to provide backup when the desk guy incited some member of the public into assault.

"Is there something I can do for—wait, did you say Martinelli? Casey Martinelli?"

Big guy, early sixties, wearing wrinkle-proof chinos and an open-necked shirt rather than a uniform. His attitude made him, if not the police chief, then at least today's ranking plainclothes officer. He clearly knew me. Or anyway, he had once.

"I go by Kate now, but yes, that's me."

He came forward hand out, face crinkled into a smile. "Dan Ruckart. We went to school together, back when dinosaurs walked the earth."

His grip was enthusiastic, and his face and name began to ring distant bells: older than me, but close enough to have overlapped in high school. He'd been a football player, popular but not a jerk with it. Though why a varsity football player would remember a girl on the softball team I couldn't think. We sure hadn't moved in the same circles.

"Dan, yes. How *are* you? You're looking great!"

He laughed. "I'm looking like a linebacker gone to seed, but you don't even have much gray in your hair."

"I think you need glasses, Dan."

"Come on in."

I followed him, doing the usual cop's survey of his office on the way: family pictures on the desk, handshake pictures on the wall, some framed letters and awards. But in addition to the expected—formal portraits of President Obama and Governor Brown, a grinning mayor and some Lion's Club fundraisers—one big framed photograph showed a Habitat for Humanity project with Dan Ruckart in a well-used tool belt, and another had large, white Dan Ruckart surrounded by a mostly brown kids' soccer team, everyone wearing wide grins.

I gestured at the soccer photo as I sat down. "Looks like you changed football for *fútbol*."

"Yeah, soccer's a great game. Way more running up and down for the coach, which keeps my wife and doctor happy. So, what can the Diamond Lake Police Department do for the famous Inspector Kate Martinelli?"

That explained it: he'd seen me on the news, some prominent case or other. At least there was no resentment in his voice, no patriarchal jolliness.

"I'm not here with the Department, just a private citizen. I was hoping that Diamond Lake keeps old accident reports. Very old. Like, 1983."

"Nineteen eight—ah. This'll be your sister?"

I was surprised. "You knew Patty?"

"Nah, she was a lot younger'n me, and I wasn't even in Diamond Lake when she died. First college, then Germany with the Army," he explained. "But, well, there's only two famous people ever came from this town, and you're one of them."

"Famous? So… people here all know about me?" That wasn't creepy at all.

"Oh not really, I didn't mean that. It was just, a while back, after some interview with you on the tv, the guys were talking about how you grew up here, out where the mall is now, but that you didn't have any reason to come back because your mother died, and before that your sister went in a car crash."

"Well, I'm glad I don't have to worry about Diamond Lake stalkers. Anyway, I had to come through town for a witness statement, and Patty's accident was something I'd always meant to look into." As I said it, I heard how thin an excuse it was. A police chief might need more than a colleague's mild curiosity to justify spending city money on a clerk digging through the records. "But, you know, a stupid accident—it never seemed like something that needed explaining. Then the other day my daughter did a Google search for her aunt, and came across an article that had a heavy hint Patty committed suicide."

"And you're hoping that wasn't so?"

"I'm hoping I didn't miss something."

I watched his face go from stern to thoughtful to soft, and it occurred to me that he might think my concern was not over Patty, but Nora. I opened my mouth to clarify, then decided that if he thought I wanted to reassure a similarly at-risk daughter, he might be more inclined to help. I changed what I was going to say. "Dan, I know what records offices look like, and if they're anything like those of the SFPD, it would take a hunt. I'd be happy to go looking on my own, if that's not a problem."

It was not a problem, although he didn't turn me loose to ravage the shelves. Instead, he assigned me a clerk. "But only for an hour, I'm afraid. If the two of you can't find it by then, you'll just have to fill out a request and let us do it on our own time."

I thanked him warmly, wishing his soccer team all the best, and stood up. Then I paused. "Okay, Dan, I have to ask: who is Diamond Lake's other 'famous person'?"

"Mark Fields, of course."

My reaction to the name confirmed that there was some complex bit of memory attached to that person, though the near-panic I had felt in front of the school was now a sort of general disgust. Like seeing the name of a town that is both familiar and troubling, which you later discover you know from headlines after a mass shooting.

Not that a town would name a high school building after a criminal. It must be a coincidence, a local benefactor whose name happened to trigger a cop's response. Had to feel sorry for the local guy.

"Yes, I saw the name on the high school, but I couldn't—"

"*The* Mark Fields. 'Tech Guy'? 'More apps than Apple'? That Mark Fields."

"I've heard of Tech Guy, sure, but I guess I didn't know who that was. He comes from Diamond Lake?"

"Seems unlikely, doesn't it? But then, he wasn't actually born here, he came when he was little. But I'd have thought you two were in high school together. What year did you graduate?"

"Eighty-one."

"So maybe he was a couple of years after you. And maybe you went to different elementaries and junior highs—he lived north of town. But you'd have met him, high school wasn't that big—I'm a little surprised you didn't recognize his name. He's in the alumni news all the time."

I didn't point out that not all graduates of Diamond Lake High were signed up for its newsletter.

"Well, Dan, you know how that age is—if you're in different groups, you might as well live on different worlds." And I didn't need to remember the Fields boy to know that he'd been one of the In Crowd: if the Fields family lived in what we called north-town, they had money.

"Ain't that the truth? Still, it would've been nice to know what he was going to do when he grew up, so we all could have invested in him and retired years ago."

I laughed politely along with the chief.

"Anyway," he said, "you want to look at our records. Let me tell them you're coming."

He picked up the phone and explained to the person on the end who I was and what I needed, then stood up and shook my hand.

"All set. Try not to keep her more than an hour or so."

"I'll do my best. Thanks so much, Dan. I'll let you know if I find anything."

"Good luck."

And off I went to do battle with the dusty files.

V

In the end, the Diamond Lake records offices were so bizarrely well organized, the clerk and I were in and out in fifty-three minutes—and that included a stop at the printer so I could take the file with me. There wasn't even a disgusting amount of dust on the folders.

Somewhat stunned, I pulled out my phone to check the time. Not even 3:30—*oh crap*, I thought: *the parking meter.*

It showed expired, as it must have for at least twenty minutes. Fortunately, the department's parking control officer was not as efficient as its records office, and there was no ticket under my wiper blades. I climbed into the car, tossing the folder on the passenger seat to check my cell for messages.

When I had dealt with a couple of emails and had a text exchange with my partner about a case we were working, it was nearly 4:00. If I left now, I'd be back for the end of dinner, as I'd semi-promised. Or not, depending on whether the rush hour traffic was merely awful or truly horrendous. My thumb hovered over Lee's name on the text bar, but I then closed it out and phoned her instead.

"Hi sweetie," she answered.

"How're things?"

"Same old. Nora went over to Yaz's so they could work on that history project, she may stay for dinner."

31

It was on the tip of my tongue to ask if she was sure Nora was with her friend and not sneaking off with The Boy, but I caught it back. Kate, don't be That Mother.

"Yeah, about dinner. Even if I leave now, I may be late."

"'Even if?' You have other things you want to do out there in the sticks?"

"Well, for one thing I need to pee."

She laughed. "And while you're in peeing you might as well talk to John Smith and Jane Doe, I know. Listen, sweetheart, take your time. Don't leave till you're satisfied. It'll bug the hell out of you if you don't."

"Man. You are so clever. You should've been a therapist or something."

"Or something. Honestly, Kate, I'm fine, there's leftovers, and Yaz's mom has to go out anyway so she'll drop Nora off. If you wait a while, the drive will take half as long."

"Well, if you're sure."

"How is it, being there?"

"A weird mix of boringly familiar and completely unexpected."

"But not unpleasant?"

"Not as bad as I thought it would be."

"Have you gone past your house?"

"Where it was, you mean? No. I don't think I will. But I did drive past the place Patty died." She made a sound, of sympathetic pain. "And I managed to get a copy of the accident report."

"Have you read it?"

"Not yet."

"You're sure you want to?"

"I think I need to."

"I understand. I'll have my phone on me, in case you want to talk. And I'll be up when you get in."

"Love you," I told her.

"Me too, you."

I slipped the phone into my pocket, and gazed across the sidewalk at one of the more familiar storefronts in the town. Its paint was new and the sign was a slightly retro version of the one it had worn thirty years ago, but the teasing odors were precisely the same.

They also reminded me that I hadn't eaten since breakfast. And the sign said it was open until five. I slipped a few more quarters into the parking meter and went through the door of the Village Bakery—where the old-fashioned bell that jangled a welcome instantly transported me into one of the few good corners of my childhood. The bakery and library had been my two places of comfort. I had spent countless afternoons here, bent over a library book, eking out my single cup of cocoa and a sweet of some kind.

To my shock, the very same woman looked up from behind the counter—but no, this was not time travel. Her blue eyes and greying red hair were also on the framed photograph on the wall behind her. This would be the next generation of bakers. Who was watching me dubiously as I stood in the doorway, grinning like a lunatic.

"I used to come here when I was a kid," I explained. "Is that your mother's picture?"

Her face relaxed. "It is. She retired a few years ago, though she still comes in when things are busy."

"Well, tell her an old customer said hi. Can I have a coffee, and maybe one of those?"

The object was a softball-sized muffin with nuts on top, which barely fit on the plate she put onto a tray with the coffee. Before she rang it up, I asked if she could arrange a thank-you box of cookies to be sent across to the police department, and she said sure, as if it were a regular occurrence.

She even gave me a price break on everything, being the end of the day.

The bakery's seats had changed, but the new owner had kept the banquette seating along the sides, and I slid into roughly the same place that I'd treasured as a child—though with very different reading material.

The accident report form was as bland as they come, with time of day, condition of road, vehicle involved, and so on. As I'd imagined (remembered?) it was an old car, which probably meant worn tires and loose steering.

The road sketch was hand-drawn rather than computer-generated, but it was clear enough. Because this crash involved a fatality, it received greater follow-up than a mere injury or property damage. Someone had even closed the road long enough to measure and photograph the skid marks by daylight. I suspected that a number of the photos in the file—which the clerk had made in color, then fastened together with a big clip—would be of the road itself, but I left those for the moment.

It appeared that Patty had been driving along Pipeline Road just before midnight, going at least fifty mph, which was twenty over the posted limit. Just before one of the road's gentle left-hand curves, she jerked the wheel to the right, then an instant later, slammed on the brakes and yanked the wheel back to the left. The tires, whose tread someone had bothered to measure, were perfectly serviceable, but not good enough to hang onto the road. The vehicle was travelling sideways when it hit one of those massive eucalyptus trees, its point of impact halfway along the passenger side. Both windows on that side exploded outward. The car's steel frame actually bent several degrees around the tree.

The written report that followed gave greater detail. The car was fifteen years old, and belonged to a classmate of Patty's, a Junior named Tony Cardone. In his interview, he referred to it as a classic, which he'd bought as a project to restore. That explained why a kid from north-town was driving a clunker. He and Patty had both been at a party that night and she'd more or less helped herself to his keys, saying she wanted some air and that she'd be back in an hour. And he was drunk enough to say sure.

Tony was adamant that he and his car were not to blame. The steering was fine, headlight bulbs new, tires okay. Some previous owner had even upgraded to shoulder-belts in the front. It wasn't his fault. And he'd thought she had a license. The report ended with the note that he had been crying during most of the interview.

The statement answered my earlier question: yes, the car had seat belts—and not just lap belts, but the modern three-point kind. Patty was not wearing hers. The report stated that the mechanism had been tested, and apparently all of them, while somewhat loose in their retractors, had functional clasps. Patty was across the car from the point of impact. If she'd been wearing her belt, she might have survived. Instead, the force had ripped her hands off the steering wheel and thrown her along the bench seat into the tree. The rescue crew had to cut off her shoe to free her right foot from a fold of metal.

But by then, she was long dead.

Emergency crews were on the scene within ten minutes, since the noise of the crash woke up the farmer half a mile down the road. Joseph Weber's statement was the next document in the file, written in his own hand two days after the accident—though I thought the last three sentences felt like afterthoughts, added when the investigator asked for clarification.

∽

My wife heard the sound just before midnight. We'd been asleep for a couple hours when something woke us up, and I said, Was that a crash? And she said she thought there had been a screech of brakes though I didn't hear that. And she said should I call 911? And I said maybe I should go see first, but when we looked out the window we could see lights down the road a ways. They weren't moving. So I put on my pants and boots and got the big flashlight, but she said she wasn't going to wait, what if there was somebody hurt.

When I got there I could see it was a real mess. There was glass all over the road and closer up I could hear dripping. I kept back until I could shine my light under the car, but when I saw it was the radiator leaking and not gas, I went up and looked through the missing window.

There was a girl in there, sitting on the passenger side but stretched out across the seat like she was reaching for the driver's door. I couldn't see her face, just the back of her hair, but there was blood in it and she was lying real still. I was going to reach inside to feel her wrist, but just then I heard the first sirens coming so I figured it was better to wait til the ambulance came, to be sure.

I got there probably six or seven minutes after we heard the crash. The cops were there a couple minutes later.

I didn't smell any alcohol or drugs, just the hot engine and the radiator fluid.

I had one of the dogs with me, on a lead so I could keep him out of trouble, and when we were waiting for the sirens he started barking off at the fields. I remembered it the next day, and I took my dog back in case the girl had hit a deer or something, but if so it must have got away since my dog didn't find it.

❧

The next thing in the file was the autopsy.

No way I wanted to look at that. No way I could avoid it.

I took another swallow of the now-cold coffee, wishing it was something a lot stronger, but before I could start that dark task, I was interrupted by a wave of happy young voices.

I looked up in surprise as half a dozen school-age girls came tumbling into the bakery, phones in hand and backpacks over shoulders. They greeted the red-haired woman with the kind of cheerful politeness used for a friend's mother—and since one of the girls had hair that same red color, it wasn't hard to pick out which. The mom handed out drinks and substantial muffins without ringing anything up, which confirmed matters.

They were younger than Nora, maybe thirteen. Hence the backpacks—those would disappear in high school, when the girls suddenly became too cool to admit to homework and textbooks.

They hung around in front of the display case, giggling and exclaiming over some incident at school, then took their whipped cream-laden drinks to a nearby table. Closing the file cover over the photographs, and checking to make sure no curious eyes could see the pages, I opened the autopsy report and started reading, accompanied by the kind of conversation you might expect from a group of heterosexual thirteen-year-old girls.

Meanwhile, the brutal print phrases flowed past my eyes: "soft tissue hemorrhage" and "considerable bruising" and "fractures of the two external metatarsals"; the broken nose, thumb, and collarbone; the fact that she was not a virgin, and that she was not pregnant.

Immediate cause of death, the coroner found, was suffocation, possibly due to her lying face-down and unconscious against the seat. At least two other injuries were severe enough to have been life-threatening.

A note under Distinguishing Marks caught my eye: she'd had a tattoo. A daisy, just above her left ankle.

Thirty years ago, tattoos were a clear declaration of rebellion and wickedness—but a daisy? Oh, Patty.

The coroner's sketched figures (I lifted that page up from the table, to be sure no innocent gaze fell on it) gave details of her injuries: mostly, as one might expect, on the right side of her body, from trapped foot to cracked skull. But her nose was broken as well. I looked back at the written description, and saw that yes, assuming I remembered the difference between temporal and parietal bones, the chief impact was just above and behind her right ear. Something else had hit her face as she was thrown around. The combination of swollen nose and a jaw shoved closed against the seat meant that once unconscious, she had no air.

I braced myself, and reached back into the folder for the photos.

These were arranged in the order the police photographer had shot them, although this had to be a selection from several rolls of film. The first was taken through the open door, and showed Patty sprawled across the car's old fashioned bench-style seat. As Joseph Weber had said, her left arm was stretched toward the camera, fingers just touching the edge of the upholstery. Her face was pressed into the seat, but her right hand, which should have slumped to the floor, was stretched back as if reaching behind her. It was hard to tell, but it looked as if she was wearing that heavy cuff bracelet she liked, and it had caught on the strap of the seat belt. But she'd been driving. Why was her arm through that side's belt?

I stared out the window for a while, constructing an explanation in my mind's eye. Worn retractors on the belts. Left hand one way, right hand the other.

She'd had one split second of knowing: the car was going into that tree. She threw up her right arm in reaction, but her body must have been swiveling as well in that last instant. Instead of her braced arm meeting the tree, it was swinging forward, just enough to slip inside the loosely hanging passenger belt. She hit, then fell sideways onto the seat, leaving her wrist caught on the strap.

I pulled my eyes away from the all-too-clear figure to look at the rest of what the camera had caught. The flash washed out the door-frame, but there were marks in the paint. I squinted, then turned back to the report to check.

Yes: the first police responder had to pry the driver's door open, using a crow-bar from his trunk kit that left gouges on the frame. When the paramedics arrived, they'd made no attempt at removal or resuscitation, merely confirmed her dead and stood back to let the police take over.

The photos were puzzling, parts of a story that failed to come together. Her left arm bothered me, stretched out along the seat. I'd have guessed it was pulled out from underneath her, yet both Joseph Weber and the paramedics stated it was that way when they first saw her. So unless Weber lied... But why would he? No one could blame him for trying to help an injured girl.

I replayed the motions in my mind, trying to find a sequence that would leave her in that position. If her left arm, after her hands were torn from the steering wheel in the skid, was rigid and outstretched when she hit the tree, it could have remained in that position. Although a person would think that if she'd been instantly knocked out, her arm would have been trapped under her slumping body.

Unless Patty was not knocked out. I had a brief, queasy vision of my dying, blood-drenched sister using her last conscious thought to claw her fingers along the glass-strewn seat toward the door... and I quickly turned to the next photograph.

This shot showed her trapped right foot, taken before the crew cut into her shoe. Next came a pair of awkward photographs, with the camera held against the roof of the car, aiming down. Overlapping the two gave the entire front seat up to the window. It showed how even the comparatively massive sixties steel frame hadn't kept the tree from shoving into the body of the car, moving the seat-back forward a few inches. Patty lay tucked beneath the forward-leaning seatback, her jeans, shoulders, and hair glittering with crumbles of glass. Her face was hidden, for which I was grateful. The autopsy's description of the amount of glass embedded in her right cheek was vivid enough for my mind's eye.

The rest of the pictures had been taken by daylight. The first showed the car in situ, after Patty was taken away. For it, the photographer had retreated across the road to get a bumper-to-bumper view. The door was not quite shut—I doubted the mechanism would latch any more—but showed what the car looked like when the first patrolman arrived. The photographer must have been more or less standing in the drainage ditch, putting the lens slightly below the level of the car's roof. The wide picture showed the road covered with broken glass and the side of the car with its driver's window missing. The window behind it was a spiderweb of cracks. In the background, blunt and monstrous, loomed the old tree.

The next photograph was taken after the car was towed. Markers stood near the skid lines that swerved first one way, then the other, before dissolving into the chewed-up gravel at the side. The tree showed a pale chunk bitten out of it, just above the gouged earth and scraps of car. An old rag lay trodden under many feet. In the grass lay a shoe, the leather sawed down to the instep.

Something about the glass seemed odd. And the rag—why did it look so naked? Not that it looked arranged there, or out of place, but... Then I saw it: most of the scenes I'd walked around were littered with the debris of paramedics, all kinds of blood-stained scraps and discarded wrappers testifying to their desperate attempts to staunch a wound, save a life.

Not here.

The girls finished their high-calorie coffee drinks (decaffeinated, if I judged the mother correctly) and dispersed with much hugging and exclaiming. The woman brought me a fresh coffee, by way of apology for the racket, glancing curiously at the pages that I'd taken care to cover completely as the pack drifted by.

"Sorry if the girls disturbed your reading."

"Oh, no," I assured her. "I've got one of my own just a little older—I always like it when she brings a gaggle of friends home."

"It's a blessing when they don't mind being under a mother's eye."

"It is indeed."

When she was gone, I looked at the last two photographs in the stack. One showed a close-up of the driver's window. Jagged reflections in the bottom track confirmed that the glass was broken out, not simply rolled down. A thin kink of thread descended from one corner. Greasy blotches stained the paint around the missing window.

The final photograph showed the steering wheel and dash board. Having lived with crime scene investigations, I knew I was looking at fingerprint powder here, not dirt—then I flipped back to the previous shot, and decided that what I had taken for grease was the same black powder. Rural police, fingerprinting a car stolen by the person who died driving it? That seemed remarkably scrupulous. And the report said that most of the prints belonged to the deceased, Patricia Martinelli. Except, surely that was wrong? This wasn't Patty's car. Her prints should have been in the minority.

I went back to the initial report, wondering if I'd missed something, but there was no explanation of why they'd decided to dust it for prints, or what conclusion they had reached. It did seem to me that the pattern of print powder on the wheel was a bit odd, but in the end, I shook my head.

I'd worked in a big city force too long, where budget overruled most other considerations. Maybe the police here, faced with the death of a teenager, had automatically launched into the full spectrum of response before realizing that the only crime involved was theft of an old car—and not even that, once they found she'd had permission. Maybe they were bored. Or the chief took advantage of the crash as an exercise in evidence-gathering. Which clearly they needed, if those print-free areas on the paint and steering wheel had come about by uniforms carelessly rubbing against them.

I couldn't see that it mattered, one way or the other.

It was nearly five, and the bakery's owner had been cleaning up for some time. I used the restroom, thanked her for her table—and bought her last half-dozen cookies to take home with me.

I sent Lee a text, then started the car.

But instead of turning toward the freeway, I made a U-turn and headed back to Pipeline Road.

This time, even though thirty years of growth had come between the photograph and the reality, I had no trouble spotting the tree.

I pulled over, turned off the engine, got out—and was shocked when the smell of death washed over me.

An instant later, I realized it was not the actual smell of death, but the chest rub that cops use to smother the stench of decomp. Vicks smells like eucalyptus trees. (And yes, every time we treat our kids for colds, we wince.)

Now that I'd seen the photographs, I knew which tree had killed her: the one just after the gap for access to the field. The wound in its massive trunk had long healed over, but the tree would never lose the scar.

The air did not move. Cows grumbled in a distant field. A small plane passed overhead. If she'd swerved a split second earlier, she could have missed it entirely.

Patty, what the hell were you doing down here? What made you jerk the wheel like that? The glow of a cat's eyes? A flash of headlights from around the corner? Was someone walking along the pavement?

With the sun going low and no breath of wind to stir the silvery leaves, the trees no longer seemed lovely. They towered above me, huge, silent rulers of everything in sight. Nothing grew around their bases. No birds sang from their branches. The stink of them rose up in my throat and made me gag.

I wanted to take a chain saw to the fucker, to fell it with an earth-thundering crash. Cut it apart, burn it to ash, poison its roots and grind its stump to the ground, giving this small patch of roadside back to the native oaks and blackberries.

I wanted that tree dead and gone. Instead, I got back behind the wheel and continued along the road, past the fences and the house whose mailbox still said Weber, down to the No Trespassing signs and the derelict quarry. There I turned and drove back up Pipeline Road, then through Diamond Lake to the freeway.

If I never came back to this place, it would be too soon.

∾

My sister's death was not a case. It was not even a homicide—and yet my mind set about shaping the accident as if it were. After a lifetime of habit, this was how I thought: fit all the pieces together into a story, and fret over any part that didn't fit smoothly.

As night fell and I drove across the middle of California, I turned the reports and statements and images into a story. The story of how Patty Martinelli died.

∿

The car is driving too fast on Pipeline Road, along a straightaway but coming up to a curve, when the girl behind the wheel loses control of the vehicle. She has been at a party, and though she's not drunk—blood tests will show that, eventually—she is slightly buzzed. Or it could simply be that she's in an elevated mood, after a high-spirited party followed by an illegal drive in a friend's borrowed car. She is alone, but she is relishing her daring, grown-up act of freedom. Driving, without a license—and to hell with a seat belt!

She accelerates in the dark, and is going nearly twice the posted limit on the narrow rural road when something startles her. She swerves, tries to correct, slams her foot on the brakes, and loses control, sending the heavy car into a skid. Her headlights flash across a solid wall of bark. She throws out her right hand, as if her bones might hold off two tons of violence.

The car hits the tree. The impact rips her left hand from the wheel and throws her down the length of the bench seat. In passing, some heavy object—the steering wheel? Her own hand?—hits her face, breaking her nose. The car's spin has pulled at her torso, causing the outstretched hand to slip beneath the loose strap of the shoulder belt. When she smashes into the crumpled metal and tree bark, her collarbone, skull, and thumb shatter. Shards of safety glass are driven into the skin of her face and neck. If she is not dead in that moment, she will be very soon.

The motor stalls, radiator fluid sprays, the car rocks to a halt. Seconds—minutes?—later, her body slumps down onto the bench seat, her left arm outstretched, either in a fluke of gravity and position or a last, half-conscious effort to reach for the door. As her traumatized brain goes dark, her body settles forward even more, left arm into the meeting place between seat and seat back, right hand stretched back to where her heavy bracelet has caught in the shoulder strap. The weight of her head presses her chin against the car seat, pushing her jaws together. She cannot draw breath through her mouth. The swelling in her broken nose permits no air, either. For all her injuries, all of the things that might have seen her on a surgical table for the remainder of the night, it is a simple lack of oxygen that causes Patricia Martinelli to slip away for good.

☙

My sister's death was not suicide—not unless adolescent stupidity was suicidal.

And yet…

When I got off the freeway, I pulled into a deserted parking lot to take another look through the photos. The sparkling glass. The trapped foot. The outstretched hand.

Thoughtfully, I clipped the pictures together again, shoved them back in the folder, turned off the overhead light, reached for the key… and sat.

That glass. Something was not right about the glass.

With a sigh, I let go of the key and picked up my phone instead.

"Al? This is Kate. No, everything's fine, I'd just like you to look at a file for me. Hah! No, nothing to do with Nora's boyfriend. It's… well, I suppose you'd have to call it a cold case."

VI

Tuesday morning, I detoured past the Cold Case unit and found Al poking at a sputtering coffee machine.

"You've gone high tech with your coffee," I noted. It was one of those single-cup machines that takes a plastic pod, a technique that made Lee despair for the soul of the nation.

"The thing seems to have something in its throat," he said. "I put it on ten minutes ago."

He peered at the half-inch of coffee in the cup, and I handed him some paper towels to mop away the drops sprayed in all directions.

"You probably should start over with a fresh pod."

"Do you have one of these things?" He pressed the button that opened the top, sending another mist of droplets all over.

"I wouldn't dare. Lee swears the coffee tastes like dirt, and Nora says we're drowning in plastic. I brought you the file."

"Have a seat, you can tell me what you're looking for while I try and coax this thing into giving you a cup."

"Actually, I'd rather have you look at the file before we talk. Anything I say would influence you, one way or the other. Take your time, think it over. There's certainly no rush."

"One of the advantages of working this unit," he agreed, and took the folder.

"Give me a call," I said.

"You can buy me lunch."

But I paused in the doorway to look back. As I knew he would, he'd automatically flipped open the cover and read the name. His head came up, eyebrows raised. I nodded.

"Yeah. My kid sister."

❧

At my desk, I checked the VIN for the car she'd been driving, confirmed that it had been junked two months after the wreck, and sent Al an email with that information. Then I turned to my actual work.

I didn't hear from him the rest of the day. I told myself this was a good sign, that he was spending enough time to read through the folder with care, but I knew Al too well for that. If he didn't call and tell me to stand down, it meant there was something in the reports that bugged him, too.

I didn't even consider the possibility that he'd been too busy to look at it. Al would look at something from me if he was in traction, or headed for surgery, or on a plane to Fiji with Jani.

His call came at 10:30 the next morning, from his personal phone to mine.

"Hey," I greeted him.

"Lunch?" was all he said.

"I'm free at one."

"Toby's at half past."

"You sure?"

"Just don't tell Jani," he ordered. And hung up.

Toby's wasn't actually called that—a snitch by that name used to meet us there, because it wasn't a place cops used. Which was also why Al and I would meet there if we were working on something of our own.

Plus that, the food was good and greasy and hot enough to clear sinuses.

We ordered—Al, to my surprise, going with a salad instead of the greasy end of the menu—and caught up on family news: his wife

Jani's health after a worrying test result, son Daniel's second year at Cal, and daughter Maya's choice of grad school in Germany, where they'd never see her. Jani's first child, his adopted daughter, Jules, looked to be making partner soon in her law firm. "She'd be there already if she didn't insist on spending so much time doing pro bono work for environmental groups."

"She's something else."

"Probably be mayor by the time she's forty."

"Next stop, the White House—now that Hilary's clearing the way for women in the Oval Office."

"And speaking of family."

"Patty."

"What made you go looking?"

"Nora. My own fault—I said something about Patty, and Nora was on it in a flash. The accident was so long ago, I never questioned it. My sister dies in a stupid car wreck, sadness all around, end of story. But then Nora did a search online and came up with that second 'Accident Puzzler' article."

"The one that said drugs were not an issue?"

"Right. And when I read the thing, it sounded to me like they were trying to sneak in the idea that she'd committed suicide. You know: sober driver plus fatal crash plus no seat belt plus Catholic funeral equals knowing looks. Then I thought, no, I'm reading way too much into it—but when I happened to be near Diamond Lake for a witness statement, I stopped in to talk with the police chief, who let me copy the file, and little things just, I don't know. Kept bothering me?"

Al reached down to the ancient brief-case he'd used for as long as I'd known him, coming out with a single sheet of paper covered with his small handwriting. He put it on the table between us.

"Little things like this?" The page said:

FOLLOW-UP QUESTIONS:

Who was at the party that night? Did anyone leave at the same time?

Did Patricia M have a boy/girl friend?
Was the car's fender checked? Deer blood/signs of impact?
What broke the driver's window? Impact or first responder?
Would the ME expect to see trauma on the left hand?
When did Joseph Weber's dog start to bark?
Any chance Weber reached in, brushed the car, moved the arm?
Were there other photos—seat belt, fingerprints, driver's seat?
Were measurements made—driver's mirrors, seat position?
Was PM's shoe <u>caught</u>, or <u>trapped</u>?

RECOMMEND:

Forensic accident reconstruction
Medical Examiner review
Review of any materials in police storage
Interview surviving family and friends
Re-interview Tony Cardone: had he washed the car before?
Follow-up interviews with Joseph Weber, Henry Belmonte

His list was almost identical to the one in my head. I laid the page back onto the table, and was startled to see a smear of blood—no. Only tomato sauce. I picked up some napkins, aware that my heart was doing something odd. "You agree—that the accident needs a closer look."

"It may be nothing. But yes, there are some troubling questions. I have a guy I want to send it to."

"Not our own?" The Hit and Run unit, naturally, had a trained reconstructionist, but they were as backed up as any other unit in the department.

"My guy's private, but he owes me."

"You don't want to create a case out of this, first?"

"Let's not worry about it until we get a few of those questions answered."

Such as: Was there any evidence, either physical or from the first witness, that the car had hit something?

And: Why did the driver's side window fall out onto the road, away from the tree, when everything else in the car had been thrown toward it?

And: Was her shoe trapped, or merely caught?

And: Had the car been recently cleaned? If not, why were the wheel, gear shift, and window surround free of prints?

All of which amounted to: Did the physical evidence, the victim profile, and the statements of witnesses all fit the theory that Patricia Martinelli had borrowed a car, gone for a joy-ride, and killed herself against a tree?

I glanced down at Al's list. "Who's Henry Belmonte?"

"Investigating officer. Long retired, but still in the area. I have an appointment at ten-thirty tomorrow. Want to go?"

I met his eyes, which were shining with that familiar blue they took on when he was on the chase.

"Al, this is an accident that killed a girl thirty years ago. Surely you have better things to do than drive to Diamond Lake?"

"This is your sister. So, no, I got nothing better to do."

I hadn't worked a case with Al for so long, I'd almost forgotten how much I missed it. I felt—not happy, exactly, but invigorated. Eager. I found I was grinning, even though this was my sister we were talking about.

"Well, it's your time to waste. And I know a place down there with decent coffee and great muffins."

VII

A sense of déjà vu rode with us down to Diamond Lake. My very first case with Al Hawkin—the one that had ended with a gunman at my door—had included a drive from San Francisco into California's rural heartland. And as before, on that and on dozens that followed, I drove while Al alternated between reading and snoring.

Just because I was now 52 and he was halfway retired didn't change much. Although we did pull in to use a rest stop along the way.

As if the "Welcome to Diamond Lake" sign triggered a wake-up call, Al stirred as we went past it. We'd made good time, travelling the reverse commute traffic, so it was only a little after ten. "Want to be early," I asked, "or stop for coffee?"

He chose coffee, and set about charming the red-headed owner with his usual gruff ease. But to my surprise, he told her we'd have it in to-go cups, and then asked if she knew Henry Belmonte.

"The policeman? Well, retired now. Sure I do, though he hasn't been in for a while."

"Why don't you give us a little box of whatever he likes? I bet he misses your baking."

I watched her turn pink and bustle away, as I'd watched all kinds of women do over the years. "Al, it's a good thing you became a cop.

Otherwise the department would be getting calls from a series of old ladies you'd charmed out of their life savings."

To be fair, he was almost as good at winning over men, with an air of masculine camaraderie so strong, you could almost smell the beer and hot dogs. It worked with Belmonte himself twenty minutes after we'd left the bakery: Al thrust the pink box into my hands, strode up the walkway, and stuck out his hand the moment the old guy opened the door.

Before we had reached the living room, they were buddies for life. I half expected them to look at me to produce coffee from the kitchen—but there was a wife for that. I gave her the box and went to sit with the boys.

I'd worked with men—lots of them—for whom that ignore-the-girls scenario would be standard procedure. With Al, it was a game to win the trust of a witness. Or in this case, a first responder.

Five minutes of male bonding followed: football teams and cop life edged into the woes of budget cuts and the mixed benefits of enforced retirement. Belmonte was interested in the workings of a Cold Case unit, although Diamond Lake was too small to have one built into its budget. And he was enough of a cop to nod thoughtfully at Al's admission (rather pointed, I thought) that if the SFPD didn't pay him to do the job, he'd probably work it for free, to keep from going crazy with the boredom of retirement.

A flicker of smile on Belmonte's face gave him away: he knew he was being played, but would go along with it.

I liked him better, after that. And I would trust his instincts a bit more, as well.

Once the masculine back-slapping was over, we moved on to the reason for our presence. I opened the folder—which, had Al been a true believer in male superiority, he'd have grabbed away from me—and gave Belmonte the initial report.

The old cop sat back in his chair, the sheet in one hand and a baked good in the other—the box held croissants and macaroons, to my surprise, rather than the traditional doughnuts. He read thoroughly, all the way to his signature at its bottom.

"Yeah, I remember this. Poor kid. It was a real mess."

"She was my sister," I told him.

He looked over at Al, then back at me. "I'm not sure what you two are after. It wasn't a homicide."

"There are a few loose ends."

He turned his gaze toward Al, no doubt hoping for the what-can-you-say shrug of the beleaguered male. When he did not find it, he took a bite of his chocolate croissant, thinking about matters as he chewed.

"Well, there's almost always loose ends around accidents." Had there been a pause before that last word? As if he'd drawn quotation marks around it?

If so, Al didn't seem to notice them. "Indications of this one are, you weren't sure yourself, at first."

"What makes you think that?"

"Because you started out treating it like a crime scene. Fingerprints, loads of photos. You telling us you did that for all your crashes?"

Belmonte noticed the crumbs that had rained over his sweatshirt, and brushed them—not onto the floor for his wife to vacuum, but onto his hand, to deposit back on the plate. Another notch up in my estimation.

"No, you're right. We were short that night so I was working patrol. Happens sometime in a small department. So I was the first one on the scene, other than the guy who lived down the road. It was him who called it in. Or maybe his wife? Anyway, he was there, and it looked obvious what happened, but like you say, something about it didn't feel quite right. I never did figure out what it was, but you know how it goes: when in doubt, bring out all the guns. Anyway, we did go over the car pretty closely, and nothing showed up."

"What were you looking for? Tampering?"

"Oh no, just any kind of criminal negligence. It was a beat-up old car, and there was always a chance that her family would sue the owner. If a wheel fell off or something, you know?"

"But it didn't."

"It would be in the report."

"Do you know if there were any tests done on the front of the car, blood or hair or something, like if it hit a deer?"

"I don't think the front was damaged much. You can check on the photos."

"There's only a handful of them."

"There were more to begin with. Sorry, I guess they got thrown out."

"What about the party she'd been at? Didn't you interview the rest of the kids? Or her friends?"

"We might've talked with a few of them, but of course, it was decided pretty soon that we were looking at an accident."

"There aren't any statements from them in the file."

"Really? Sloppy bookkeeping, I guess. Or maybe because they were minors." But his eyes wouldn't meet mine. "Far as I remember, there was beer and probably some pot, and she asked one of the kids if she could borrow his car and he said sure." He shook his head. "That's all I can dredge up off-hand."

"Pipeline Road is nowhere near where we lived," I remarked.

"Yes." His expression made it clear: this was another point in favor of suicide. "Anyway, we just wanted to make sure the car itself wasn't to blame. And lab work's so expensive, when the chief decided not to spend any more, I couldn't really argue."

"But at the same time," Al pointed out, "you left all the stuff you'd pulled together in the file."

"Sure. Well, not all the stuff."

Al's coffee cup paused halfway to its saucer. "You kept other evidence?"

"I don't know if you'd call it evidence, and I doubt it's still there, but we had a box in the lock-up for years—photos, notes, stuff we picked up from inside the car. Maybe they stuck the negatives in there? Anyway, nothing very exciting. An empty beer can under the seat, couple of marijuana roaches in the ashtray. Samples of glass from the ground. I know the box was there in the nineties, because when DNA work started to get easier, I sent a couple things off to the lab, to have them checked. Like her, um, her underwear." He avoided my eyes, as if I were Patty's disapproving mother rather than her cop sister.

"Get anything?" Al asked.

"No. The only DNA was hers."

"So she probably didn't have sex that night."

"Not unless she showered after. Or used a condom. Anyway, there didn't seem to be a whole lot of time between when she'd left her party and when she hit that tree."

"Tell me about the party," I asked.

"It was just some get-together. Kids, you know?"

Al and I held our silence. Belmonte's expression became increasingly uncomfortable.

Finally, he sighed. "Tell you the truth, after all this time I couldn't say exactly where it was or who was there. But it would have been some of the kids from north-town. The Mayor's daughter was about that age, and she went through a pretty wild patch. Not that you'd know it now," he added, trying for a rueful chuckle.

"And you didn't want to put the town's rich kids on record, for holding a party that ended with a death."

"The party had nothing to do with it. She wasn't drunk, so there were no liability issues. But yeah, if we'd done formal interviews, it would've made the papers, and raised a stink about under-age drinking and kids left alone. The boy she'd borrowed the car from—name of Cardone—was a good kid, and his mother was on the City Council. She and a couple other mothers came in the next day and had a little talk with the chief, and after that he told me to close it up. If I'd had any real doubts, I'd have made a stink, but I interviewed the boy myself, and I could see how broken up he was. He ended up quitting school, joined the Marines, died in the Gulf War with a bronze star and a purple heart.

"Anyway, I kept things open for a day or two, so I could ask around, but I couldn't find any reason to dirty the reputations of a bunch of kids who'd done nothing worse than have a party with beer. Probably not how we'd do it today, but then? It happened."

"Except it didn't," I said. "From the dates in the report, you were working the case for at least two or three weeks. Why?"

He exhaled, and looked up at me. "Because I wasn't really satisfied. That it was an accident. And I wanted to know. I had a daughter two years younger, who was going through some trouble of her own."

"You thought maybe Patty committed suicide," I said.

"To be honest we all did. But it bugged me that I couldn't get a hold on why. I mean, yeah, she was having problems at home and school, but no more than any kid. And she seemed to have friends, and she was bright, she'd been talking to the school counselor about college. She wasn't pregnant. I couldn't find any of the obvious signs."

"So you went looking for some of the less obvious signs," Al finished.

"And I couldn't find any. So I decided it really had been a sad accident, and I let it go. Signed off, packed it away, let them haul the car to the junk yard."

"But it was years later that you sent her underwear in to the lab," I objected. "That doesn't sound much like letting go."

"Oh, that was something else entirely. We had a serial rapist working the area in the mid-nineties, and I thought maybe she'd been one of the early cases, so I included hers in with a couple of others. It was a stretch, and like I say, nothing came of it."

I looked over the table at Al, to see if he had anything else, then reached to gather the papers back into the folder.

"I'm sorry I couldn't help you more," Belmonte said.

"Think about the names of those kids at the party," Al suggested, his voice making it almost a command.

"I'll see what I can come up with," the other man agreed, an unspoken acknowledgment that it was wrong not to have put them into the record in the first place.

Al and I drove in silence back toward town, busy with our own thoughts. As the outskirts appeared, he spoke.

"You think the evidence locker here will be off-site?"

"The building's big enough, they might have it all under the same roof. You think we should go hunting?"

"Well, they did keep the basic file, they might have hung onto the box as well."

"You want to do that?"

"Don't you?"

"Sure—but I'd also like to see if I can come up with any names, from the time Patty was here. People who might remember her."

"School yearbooks?"

"That's what I was thinking."

"Divide and conquer? We could even be home for dinner."

Al Hawkin: eternal optimist.

I pulled into a space in front of the police department, and handed Al the keys. "If their evidence locker is elsewhere, you might need the car. Text me when you're done. If I haven't heard from you, I'll meet you here."

"I can drive you up to the school," he protested.

"Thanks, but I was hoping to avoid that particular hell."

VIII

High schools are touchy about the whole privacy thing. When cops show up at their door, principals tend to expect warrants and explanations and usually end up kicking the decision up the ladder to the district offices, and days go by.

But in a small town, the public library can be a source of everything from genealogical research to ESL classes. And the thing about public libraries is, they're public.

The face of this one had not changed since my earliest memories, although the sleek new wing tacked onto the back suggested something considerably more modern inside.

And yet when I walked up the ramp where the old building had only stairs (the Carnegie libraries not having been saddled with ADA compliance) and pushed open the doors, I might have been ten years old again.

Wooden desk, varnished wood floors, dark stacks—even the smell of it! I stopped dead in surprise, which caught the eye of the librarian behind the desk. I gave him an embarrassed smile.

"Good morning," he said. "Help you with something?"

"No, thanks," I said, continuing on as if my feet knew where they were going. Which they did, a little, although the card-catalogue was now a series of computer monitors.

In a few minutes, I was in the reference section looking at two and a half shelves filled with Diamond Lake High yearbooks. The spines grew taller, thicker, and brighter as they traveled from top left to bottom right. To my relief, the 1980s were mostly complete. I carried 1981 to 1984 to a nearby table.

I had graduated in 1981, so naturally I opened that one first. God, we were young and stupid looking. Artificial smiles, big, shiny hair down to the eyebrows for both sexes, boys in thick neckties and girls in huge turtlenecks. Glasses so big they might have had wipers attached. And everyone so white—which they weren't, not that I remembered, but looking more closely, I discovered that the black-and-white printing made Hispanic kids look pale and African-Americans look Hispanic.

And here was Katarina Martinelli, smiling out from the Senior Class section with absolutely no idea what life had in store for her. A few pages later, among the grid of smaller Freshman photos, was Patricia Martinelli: shy, clean-faced, in a shirt Mother must have chosen for her. When I flipped to the index at the back, I found only that one page number—but the name above her had two: Katarina "Casey" Martinelli also appeared on the solitary double-page display of girls' sports (compared to—I counted them—the twenty-one pages of boys' teams, from football to golf.) And most of the girls' photos were action shots showing a lot of leg.

God bless Title IX, I thought, though it took a long time to make itself felt. I pushed away my graduating year and pulled up that for 1982, Patty's second year at Diamond Lake High.

Again, the index had a single number next to her name, her formal Sophomore class portrait. I remembered the picture, probably because Mother had raised such a stink over it: Patty in raccoon-mask makeup, her hair teased and sprayed into a sculptured mound.

After a bit I leafed through other pages: stage productions, marching band, a class with its heads bent over desks, a chemical formula on a blackboard.

Reluctantly, I closed its covers and reached for 1983.

Patty's Junior-year picture was set apart from her classmates inside a black square. "In Memoriam" it said, with her dates and a bit of Khalil Gibran so trite I could just hear her snort of laughter. The photographer hadn't been able to coax a show of teeth out of her, and had settled for an expression he'd probably taken for a smile, but which I recognized as my sister's *oh-you-idiot* look, used for everyone from a scolding teacher to an irritated sister to—increasingly—a mother attempting to regain control.

She wore less makeup than she'd gotten away with in 1982, though still more than most girls on the page. She also faced the camera straight-on instead of that coy tip-of-the-head pose everyone else had been placed in. *I know what I'm doing,* her picture said. *Just don't get in my way.*

After a minute, I turned to the index, expecting nothing but that single formal portrait. Patty was not a joiner, which left out the drama, French, debate, and Pep clubs, and she'd turned her back on sports, so no Martinelli in her year of Girls' Softball—but I was surprised to find two more page numbers next to her name: one in an art class, the other among the crew in November's stage production of *Music Man,* painting a backdrop.

Art: of course.

The in-class photograph showed her alone, hair over her face as she bent over a sketch pad, framed by an out-of-focus room scattered with easels: an artsy depiction of Student at Work. The group shot was posed but more natural, and included three other girls. The two on the left had the scrubbed, wholesome look of cheerleaders. On the right were Patty and a tall blonde dressed in a polka-dot shirt and the kind of pants that could only be called "slacks." The caption gave her name as Lisa Ferraro—Italian, though she looked like an early Princess Diana, while Patty at her side might have been a high school-aged Siouxsie Sioux.

Unlikely as it would seem, my short Goth sister and the tall Princess Di-wannabe were grinning at each other like—well, like sisters, in front of their painted backdrop of a small-town library.

I wrote down the various names and took photos of the pages, then checked the index for any other appearances of Lisa Ferraro, since any girl who got that kind of expression out of my sister might know what Patty was up to, those final weeks of her life. There were no other citations of her name, but in the 1984 volume, I found Lisa Ferraro twice: among the Seniors, and again with the theater program. Did she look sad, having lost her friend Patty the previous year? She looked older, certainly. She was growing into a considerable beauty.

I'd noticed, paging through, that most of the group shots didn't bother with names. It might be worth a more methodical look.

I started with the embossed and gilded 1981. Its first half-dozen pages were in color, before reverting to the cheaper black and white. I ran my eyes over the images of innocence past, a community so young it thought parents were there to protect, that futures were open, that old was a place they'd never visit.

Had the school ever looked that welcoming, I wondered? Had our faces actually been that innocent, the teachers that friendly? Pictures lied, of course. Like this kid, shown helping a teacher set up for an after-school event: he'd been expelled for weekend vandalism. And that teacher there, showing a student how to adjust her microscope—wasn't he the one who'd been arrested for selling cocaine a few years later?

Or were those all glitches in the mental filing system? How would I know about the later scandals of Diamond Lake, anyway? Did I ever write to any friends? One or two classmates might have looked me up in Berkeley, on their way out to the bigger world, but I couldn't have told you their names. No, most of my life before my twenties—before I met Lee—was nothing but wisps and impressions.

I did possess a certain body-memory of Diamond Lake High: a corridor outside Spanish class that overlooked the parking lot; an English class I'd liked, around a corner from the main quad; the art lab there, the gym here. And when I pored over the images of my classmates, the occasional face or name carried a sort of memory of memory, as people I had known once upon a time. A few clear events did step out of the mist: here, for example, was the British exchange student who'd inadvertently convulsed the class by asking her neighbor if she could borrow his rubber. And wasn't that the cheerleader who'd burst into the restroom in mortified tears, when someone pointed out that her white jeans were now red about the crotch? And that boy, there—surely I'd seen his face above a trash-bin, stuffed there by some bonehead jocks?

The common thread here seemed to be humiliation, which made sense: humiliation was the currency high school students used to buy their way up the social ladder.

And as if the reflection served as a court summons, I turned the page and felt a jolt of electricity jerk me in my chair. *Jesus, how could I have forgotten him?*

Big, good-looking kid in a letterman jacket, whose every pore shouted family money. Football? No, track. Blue eyes, black hair, six foot, wearing a wry grin that showed teeth from an orthodontist's gallery, the tilt to his head asking, *Am I not the sexiest thing you've ever seen?*

The kind of kid who just can't believe the world doesn't want to fall in either behind him (the male half) or beneath him (the females). The kind of kid who can't quite understand the word *No*. Who takes refusal as a game, a challenge, an invitation.

I checked the section: these were 1981's sophomores. Two years behind me, but his size, athletic skill, and family money made him the natural-born king of Diamond Lake High. I, on the other hand, had been so far down in the Diamond Lake social hierarchy that it took him until the very end of my senior year to notice me, and add me to his game. Not that he'd slept with all his conquests—we all knew that he saved actual sex for the gorgeous few, rather than risk his reputation by sleeping with the dogs. It was the girls' acknowledgment that counted. As soon as a girl flirted back, showing that, sure, she might be interested, he'd drop her. Publicly, with a scornful laugh and a mental check beside her name.

Or an actual check, for all I knew.

In any event, he got around to Casey Martinelli a few weeks before graduation, and paused by the bench where I was eating lunch to perform his male-cockerel strut—only to be stunned when I gave him a glance and went back to my book.

Most young men faced with rejection would make some jokes about frigidity, and start a rumor about lesbian tendencies, then go on to other victims. Not this one.

Instead, he'd doubled down, in a way even the most insecure and naïve girl, in an age before the dangers of stalking came to light, would find first creepy, then threatening. School became a constant offensive (in both senses of the word) with charm and jokes and physical proximity. I kept my face down, avoided him when I could, and counted the days, trying not to think about how his friends had started to snicker and the rest of the school was taking note.

How could I have forgotten this? Well, I'd managed to leave behind everything else from Diamond Lake—and I suppose that this early male pushiness just sort of faded into all the years of lesbian insult and attitude. But still…

As I studied that gloating face, I realized that here was another foundation piece of my past. The episode itself had retreated behind the wall I'd built in front of childhood, but its lesson remained, the knowledge that some apparently normal people do not recognize normal limits. That I needed to be a little watchful, always, for the individual who couldn't let go, who simply *had* to win, no matter the cost. That a cop's job was to stand up and say, *Enough.*

I doubt he ever intended to rape me. If they'd been older, if it had been later in the night, if he'd happened across me alone, maybe—but as a gang, he and his friends weren't drunk enough for real trouble.

No, what he wanted was domination. To force a kiss and push his hand inside my clothes, gestures of strength that would let him cross my name off his list. But he chose a poor setting, he and his friends happened to spot me walking home after dark and drove around the block.

There were four of them, piling out of the car at the far end of the alleyway we all used as a short-cut. The road behind me had traffic, if I'd wanted to try and outrun the track star; the houses around me had lights, if I wanted to scream for help. Either would admit defeat, declaring him the winner. And yes I was frightened, but I was also a senior, with the freedom of leaving Diamond Lake in my nostrils, and I was sick and tired of the idiotic routine my friends and I had put up with, all those days of being pushed and touched and teased and laughed at until we let him take what he wanted.

The two impulses warred against each other as I watched the four boys spill out of the car and come sauntering down the alley, waiting for their prey to turn and run.

Fuck, I thought. *Oh, shit.*

I didn't turn. Instead, I moved sideways, over to a collection of builders' waste that I'd walked past every day for weeks. I threw off my backpack and grabbed a scrap length of galvanized pipe—thinner, but about the same length as a softball bat. I stepped away from the wall, and took a couple of practice swings, my heart pounding so loud I could barely hear the chorus of mocking noise my bravado raised.

The pack's hoots and catcalls were loud enough to draw attention from the neighbors, but it was also a challenge, egging their leader on. And he had no choice but to meet it.

They stopped laughing when he hit the ground. If they'd been drunker, it might have ended badly, for me and for some of them. They were just sober enough to look at the blood spattering his pristine Letterman jacket and call it quits, half-carrying him to the car.

Two days later, I graduated. The day after that, I left for my summer job in Berkeley. For weeks, I waited for some man in a uniform to come and arrest me for putting the king of Diamond Lake High in the hospital.

That uniform never appeared. I returned to Diamond Lake a bare handful of times over the next few years, but that ended with my mother's funeral. I never laid eyes on my tormenter again. I let his name and his acts fade into obscurity—until thirty years later, when a yearbook photo explained the complicated reactions that had been stirred up, first by driving past the high school's new addition, then in talking with Chief Ruckart.

That kid in the letterman jacket was Mark Fields.

IX

Mark "More Apps Than Apple" Fields only came onto the Bay Area scene during the past decade. I'd never seen him in person, his photographs were of a thinner man with a beard, and his name was generic enough that it didn't rouse my long-buried memories. Though I did have to wonder if the software billionaire ever thought about his teen-aged humiliation at the hands of a lesser mortal: a girl, one who barely registered on his gorgeousness meter, who'd got lucky with a chunk of pipe.

In truth, we were both damned lucky. I'd been amped up enough that night to swing for the bleachers—and with that thought came the nauseating sensation of my bat hitting something that was not a softball. It was amazing I hadn't killed him outright.

But nobody had ever come to question me. I've had my own personal experience with being knocked out, in a case long ago, so I knew Fields himself might never be sure what had happened to him that night. His friends must have taken him to the hospital, and they'd have told him who was responsible, but had any of them ever reported it to the police? Well, I'd never been summoned home for questioning, never been confronted by his angry father, so—no, they probably had not.

Rather than admitting a girl had bested him, he may have used the *I-walked-into-a-door* defense. No doubt his buddies teased him for a while, before letting him go back to his life—maybe just a little bit wary of girls who said *No*.

The sounds of the library trickled back to my awareness. I blinked, and turned the yearbook page. Though I did watch for that face, in the images that followed. I finished with 1981, glanced up at the clock, and turned to 1982. School dances, nerdly faculty, fund-raisers, and the Homecoming court. Two pages of yearbook staff, four of after-school clubs, and half a dozen artsy photos of class-rooms at work. Then sports, again mostly boys, and heavily slanted toward football. No Mark Fields, oddly enough, despite his earlier achievement of a letterman jacket—which I was pretty sure were only given to underclassmen good enough to make a varsity team.

I felt a stir of uneasiness. Had I hit him so hard I'd ruined his high school career? Oh, come on—this was Mark Fields, one of the richest and most powerful men in the state. Whatever I'd done to him didn't slow him down much.

On to the class of 1983. More pages, more happy young faces. Artistic close-ups of keyboards and drawing pads, a teacher in a paisley tie, couples at a school dance, an assembly with a US Senator, a shot of crowded bleachers, a group of—

Wait. I turned back, to the crowd at a basketball game. Yes, those were my sister's heavily painted eyes, distinctive even in a sea of ex-cited faces, looking down from a seat high in the stands. But she was not with Lisa Ferraro.

The boy beside her, at the end of a group of other boys, was a head taller than Patty. And though she, too, sat at the end of a row of girls, their proximity did not look like mere chance. His head was bent down so close to hers, speaking in her ear over the noise, that their dark hair seemed to blend. His arm was not across her shoul-ders—did teachers monitor against displays of affection, back in 1983?—but they were so close, it might as well have been.

I couldn't make out his face, just a shiny black jacket that had to be leather, and a full head of equally dark hair. I picked up my phone to take several shots of the image, making sure they were very clear.

Nothing caught my eye in the remainder of the volume. Nor did

I find anything among the uncaptioned shots of 1984, other than the glimpse of a tall girl with light hair who might have been Lisa Ferraro. I returned the yearbooks to their shelf, thanked the librarian, and walked back across the little park to the police station, immersed in thought.

∾

Al, almost inevitably, was in Chief Ruckart's office, the two men deep in a consideration of the Giants versus the A's. But an old, taped-up evidence box on the floor beside him showed that he'd been busy, so I did not give the boys too hard a time over their waste of publicly funded salaries.

After a final exchange of pitcher stats—Madison Bumgarner versus Sonny Gray—Al tossed me the keys and scooped up the box, following me to the parking lot. I opened the trunk so he could lock his burden inside, and got behind the wheel.

"What did you find?" I asked.

"Pretty much what you'd expect from what began as a crime scene and got downgraded to an accident." He fished out his phone to check for texts, put it away. "They started with logbook, photo records, names from passing cars, and the rest. And then about ten the next morning, it all came to a halt. They swept up, packed away the signs, put away their cameras. Though they did develop all five rolls of film—they're in the box, so we can print them up. Oh, and I told Ruckart we'd bring it all back when we're finished. Sorry if that means another trip down here for you."

"You signed for the evidence?"

"Absolutely. Though he didn't seem too keen on getting it back—I think their storage is getting full."

Signing for evidence preserved a chain of custody—though considering how long this had been treated as an accident, the chances of finding anything to change that were small. Still, habits die hard.

"Also, you can draw a line through about half the names in the original report. Including, it turns out, Joseph Weber, who died a couple years ago."

"Thirty years, that's what you expect."

"What about you?" he asked.

"Some names to follow up. A girl Patty worked with on a stage production, her art teacher, that kind of thing." I told him about Lisa Ferraro, and about the boy in the leather jacket, high in the bleachers with my sister during the final weeks of her life. "Oh, and I discovered that I knocked out Mark Fields one time. *The* Mark Fields."

"What, the tech guy? How the hell did you come to do that?"

"He went to Diamond Lake High the same time I did, though a couple years behind me. He and his buddies cornered me one night after I'd publicly turned him down, and thought they'd get back at me for the insult. Nothing drastic, just a dose of ritual humiliation, but I got my hands on a length of pipe. He didn't believe I'd use it. Until I did."

The silence from Al's side of the car went on. I glanced over and saw a peculiar expression on his face. "What?"

"The kid was out for a gang-bang and just you forgot about it? Didn't you turn him in? What kind of a childhood did you have, anyway?"

"Oh jeez, Al, it was nowhere near that serious. For me, that is—he may still have headaches." I decided not to mention Fields' absence from the sports pages for the remainder of his high school career. "Like I said, he thought he'd feel me up to prove he could, I didn't let him, game over. Plus that, I left town right after and life got busy. So yeah, I just forgot."

"Well," he said, after a minute. "Remind me never to sneak up on you."

"Better believe it," I agreed. "So, how do you want to divvy up the next steps?"

While I drove, he compiled another list and marked off who was to look into what. It was dark when I dropped him at his house and continued up the Peninsula. But once in San Francisco, I did not head directly home.

Instead, I went past Building 606—the SFPD crime labs, down in Hunters Point—to sign over the evidence box, noting that I had removed its envelope of photo negatives. Those I took to the Hall of

Justice photo lab, asking for two sets of prints. Then finally, after the end of a very long day, I drove home.

My dinner was cold, but my family was still awake: that counted as a win in my book, any day.

X

When Lee and Nora had both gone up to bed, I retrieved Patty's R-rated postscript page from my locked file cabinet. Reading it, now that I'd caught a glimpse of my sister's world, my half-serious thought that she'd been out to shock her older sister grew stronger. The PS had been in her final letter, written eighteen days before she died. And since the high school basketball season started in late November, that blurred yearbook image of a boy in a leather jacket would have been taken about the same time.

(But why did the boy have to wear the cliché black leather? If it had been denim, or plaid, or a sweatshirt, I wouldn't keep picturing my sister tucked under the possessive arm of The Fonz.)

Patty's loopy scrawl read:

Dearie KC,

Meant to send this last week and it got buried so heres an update before I send it off. Mostly I might have a new after-school job, a dumb office place but it's less hours and MORE PAY!! than the theater, so yay for that. And the hours are after school instead of nights and weekend which is like TOTALLY SICK cause I got OTHER THINGS TO DO

DURING THE NIGHTS AND WEEKENDS (nudge nudge wink wink) and no I'm not gonna tell you about those OTHER THINGS TO DO cause you'll get on the bus and come right down here and give me a lecture like The Ma does and god noze I got plenty of lectures from The Ma. (You know I hate you for going off to Berkeley without me, right? Right? And how are the hippies there in Berzerkeley, honeybun? Smokin dope right? Whattabout that history exam you spent your WHOLE CHRISTMAS VACATION on—you manage to scrape by? Cause wouldn't it be the shits to flunk out and have to come home to The Dump haha. Which is why I'll be passing ALL MY CLASSES when report cards come out, not like that's work haha.)

Anyhoo off to do OTHER THINGS for a while and fling this into the mailbox, but just so you know that your sister is being TOTALLY GOOD heres a sweet pic of the SECRET FRIEND ♥ of mine that I'm doing all those OTHER THINGS ♥♥ with, or anyway a pic with a PART of him…

Yer notty sis P ♥♥♥♥♥

The photograph was a Polaroid, for obvious reasons. I have a vivid memory of it falling out of the envelope onto my dorm room floor—and being grateful that I hadn't opened the letter in public.

The Polaroid showed a tattoo of ornate Gothic letters reading **KISS** on the left and **MY** on the right. Between the two words lay the hairy cleft of a pair of male buttocks.

I'd been outraged, that was for sure—both at the image itself, and at the idea of this *thing* in close proximity to my kid sister. That I remembered—as well as the determination to go back down to Diamond Lake for a long, stern talk with Patty about everything from birth control to self-respect. The sort of talk a mother ought to have, but I knew wouldn't happen from ours.

But the next time I rode into town, Patty lay cold inside a wooden box.

Had the boy in the leather jacket come to her funeral? I remembered Mother, closed-mouth with what the priest took for grief but which I knew was a fury of disappointment. And some of Patty's friends had been there, the girls bare of makeup, the boys plucking at borrowed neckties. Had one of those anonymous mourners been the owner of those buttocks?

Now, at the age of 52, the photograph struck me as sad. That Patty would end up with a boy whose idea of a joke was to drop trou for his girlfriend's camera. Who didn't have the nerve to introduce himself as her boyfriend at the funeral—but then, her own sister had failed her, too. I wasn't experienced enough to be alarmed by the phrase "secret friend", but I should have heard the urgency, should have responded by storming down to give her hell.

Though as I studied the faded image, I found my mouth twitching. I could just see Patty's grin of mischief as she wrapped the page around that picture and sealed the envelope. The same grin she wore when I'd find Thed Bear in a Chatty Cathy pinafore, or embroidered with a scarlet lipstick smile, or wearing a girly necklace. The Polaroid of a boy's ass was just the sort of thing she'd invent, knowing how crazy it would make me.

Of course, there was also the yearbook photo of Patty with Leather Jacket, his posture suggesting intimacy. Had I any reason to think it was the same person? Maybe I could simply tell myself it was a prank—Patty's way to move our Thed Bear competition into the grownup world, what might have been the first in a long line of elaborate adult jokes.

I slid the picture back into its risqué postscript and put them away, to a place where Nora wouldn't see either for a very long time. And then I went up to bed—carrying with me the unfortunate image of The Fonz hiking up his leather jacket to show the KISS MY ASS tattoo across his butt. Lee was still reading when I came in, and I ended up telling her about the photo and what my brain had done with it, which made her laugh and let me forget about this case that wasn't a case, at least for a few hours.

☙

The next day was full, first with things I'd put off in my preoccupation with Diamond Lake, and then with a near-fatal shooting that turned out to be an idiot discharging his handgun inside a cement garage, aiming at a rat but having the bullet ricochet into his leg. I spent part of my weekend dealing with the immediate fallout from this, and the rest of it with Lee, since Nora was off in Tahoe with friends.

Bright and early Monday morning, twin parcels from the photo lab arrived. I sent one to Al's accident reconstruction guy, then firmly locked the other set in my desk to look at later, since I had an appointment to interview the rat-shooter's wife. The shooter was going to be discharged from the hospital the next day, and the Department wanted to make sure this wasn't going to be a habit—and when the fed-up woman led us to a back room and a virtual private armory of firearms, grenades, and strange explosive devices, all neatly labeled and none with a license, that took care of the rest of the day.

I did not take the photographs home with me that night.

Tuesday morning, with the rain washing down over the dirty Hall of Justice windows, I carried the package into an unused interview room and shut the door, to go methodically through them. Five rolls of film that the Diamond Lake police had taken that day, nearly two hundred images of catastrophe, twenty-six of them showing my sister's dead body—and in the end, they told me nothing I had not known from the sample I was given in Diamond Lake.

Glass on the road. A trampled rag. The gouge in the tree. Dark fingerprints in what looked like odd places. Patty trapped under the pressed-forward seat, her arm stretched out. One photograph showed her limp fingers, revealing a chip in her incongruously pink, girly nail-polish.

I went through them all a second time before I packed them away, then sat in the silent room for a long time, head in hands.

I put the package back in my desk and told my partner I was going home sick for the rest of the day. I drove out to Ocean Beach, deserted in the rain, and walked up and down the sand until my raincoat failed and I felt that I might be able to face my family without breaking down. At home, I took a very long, very hot shower. When Lee and Nora came home, I told them we were going to dinner and a movie, school night or not.

Their exchange of glances showed they knew something was up. And their silence proved that they had already agreed not to ask. Instead, during dinner we talked about nothing much and everything important. In the dark theater, I sat between them, holding their hands from time to time. At the end of the night, neither of them asked what was wrong.

I am so incredibly lucky, to have such women in my life.

XI

Wednesday, one week after Al and I had met up for lunch at Toby's, he sent me a text just as I was dropping Nora off at school.

Car guy wants to see me at 9. You free?

By "car guy" I guessed he meant the reconstructionist. I sent back:

Pick you up at the station?

And received:

8:40

Unless he'd need a car during the day, Al tended to travel in on the commuter train. Parked up the street, I could tell when the train got in: a surge of young tech workers with phones, followed by a second tide of blue collar workers with lunchboxes, and Al.

I negotiated back into traffic and said, "Your accident guy is fast, if he's done a complete reconstruction already."

"Nah, just a prelim. But he owes me some favors, so he took a quick look before he does his full-scale write-up."

"What did he say?"

"Nothing yet, just the offer to meet. He's a funny guy, always wants a face-to-face or a phone call. I indulge him when I can. You didn't have anything this morning?"

"Nothing I couldn't move. Where are we going?"

He gave me an address not far from the department's own crime labs, a nondescript office building in the corner of an industrial area. To my amusement, the walls inside were covered with elaborately framed, artistically shot photographs of distorted front ends, tangled skid-marks, and huge vehicles in impossible positions.

"That you, Al? Be with you in a jiff," called a voice from somewhere.

"No ru—" But Al's reply was drowned by a crashing noise that trailed off into the reverberations of a spinning hubcap.

The man who came out, brushing his hands together in a gesture of satisfaction, looked like something from an old movie. Shorter than I, white hair all on end, scarlet bow tie, pink shirt, and brown corduroy pants. And, as I knew I'd see before I looked down, socks with sandals.

"Al, lovely as always. And you, my dear, we met once, I do believe, although it was long, long ago. The Impala shoved over the cliff up in the headlands. The one that caught on its rear axle? We were on opposite sides of the case."

"Oh, sure," I said, having no memory of car or man. "Kate Martinelli."

"Of course you are, and I'm Ray Schulman. Al, you're looking well, the walking regime seems to be doing you good, I ought to join you but you know how it goes, too much to do here, you'd never know I'm theoretically retired, would you—but I'd die in a week without this to keep me on my toes, now where did I put your file?"

The bumbling was an act, or a defensive construct, because there was just as much confusion in his hands as there was in his dark little eyes—namely, none at all. He laid his hand instantly on what he needed, and dropped it onto the high desk facing the right way, cover already coming open. "Yes, yes," he muttered, "speed limit... point of impact... yaw marks.... shoe...."

He closed the cover and tapped it with his finger a few times, but when he looked up, there was no hesitation in his face.

"Al, you seem to be under the impression that this young lady was driving the car when it went into that tree."

"That's what they said."

"If so," said the expert firmly, "then she was steering from the passenger seat."

XII

Nearly an hour later, we walked out of the reconstruction offices. Al steered me to a coffee house, leaving me at a table while he went off to fetch drinks. He put them on the table and sat down, saying nothing.

"Your man Ray is nuts," I told him.

"True, but I've never known him get a reconstruction wrong."

"Al, he's barely looked at it."

"You want to wait till he has?"

"So it wasn't suicide. She was aiming at the gate, not the tree."

"Kate, that driver's side glass bothered both of us from the start. If Weber or Belmonte didn't knock it out, who did?"

"Some homeless guy? Who first causes the accident and then decides to steal her purse? Anyway, I don't know that we should trust Weber's statement. You know how witnesses forget things—and he's sure to have seen the road with the glass all over it the next day, after everyone from paramedics to the tow-truck driver had kicked it around. Easy to remember it like that from the beginning."

"Then what about the car seat and mirrors? And those prints on the wheel?"

The seat and the side mirror had been adjusted for a driver at least six feet tall: Patty was barely five and a half, and the car's owner,

Tony Cardone, was listed as 5'8". And one of the crime-scene photographs—only one—showed three smeared partial prints from Patty's left hand in what Ray noted was an unlikely place. Officer Belmonte, back in 1983, had been meticulous at dusting them, taking pictures, recording them onto cards, then putting them away with all the other half-processed evidence when his boss decided that the death was an accident.

"Maybe she didn't know how to adjust the seat. That could even have been the cause of the accident, that she couldn't reach the pedals. And those three smeared partials, they could be anything. Like she, I don't know, held onto the steering wheel while she was stretching to wind up the far window. Or she started out in the passenger side—they did find her left thumb-print on that seatbelt button—and then used the wheel to pull herself over to drive. Anything."

"And the fact that there were no right-hand prints at all?"

The unanswerable question: why would a car's driver leave no right-hand prints on wheel, seat belt clasp, or radio controls, but plenty of left hand ones? It wasn't like she'd been wearing one glove, or had her arm in a cast.

I took a drink of the coffee, put down the cup, and looked up at him. "Okay. So what have we got here?"

"We've got a passenger who died, and a driver who fled the scene."

"Doesn't felony hit-and-run usually involve someone outside the car?"

"Not sure it matters."

"No DA's going to prosecute it after thirty years." Back in 1983, sure—I'd imagine a rural District Attorney would happily lock away The Fonz for causing a girl's death. But the kid in the leather jacket would be in his late forties now, and what would be the point in going after some upstanding citizen for an act of adolescent cowardice?

"That would depend on Ray's final decision about those smeared prints. If it's just a felony hit-and-run, probably not. But what if his report says that your sister grabbed the wheel in a panic, and tried to steer it off the road?"

Because that was one possible explanation for those three smeared prints: that Patty was being driven along Pipeline Road against her will. That Patty tried to stop the car, either because she was being abducted, or because she'd realized that her driver was dangerously drunk or high.

Of course, the other possible explanation for her grabbing the wheel took us back to where I had first come in: a suicide attempt, by a young girl too troubled by her life to continue with it.

❧

The car is driving at high speed along Pipeline Road, too fast for the upcoming curve, when the girl in the passenger seat pops her seat belt clasp (leaving a print of her left thumb behind). She braces her right foot against the door. Before the nylon strap of the belt has pulled all the way back from her right shoulder, she lunges forward to grab the steering wheel. Her left hand clamps around the hard surface and yanks it to the right.

For a brief moment, the car is aimed at the flimsy metal gate and the field beyond. The worn tires begin to slip, threatening a spin and a driver's-side smash into the century-old eucalyptus tree. But before the spin is fully established, the steering wheel jerks back to the left and the brakes slam on. The front of the car tries to reverse direction, sending the heavy chassis into an uncontrolled skid.

The girl's hand is torn from the wheel (leaving behind three smeared prints) either because the abrupt change throws her off, or because the driver's arm swings out and smashes into her face. A split second after she hits the passenger-side door, the car meets the tree. Glass from the passenger windows explodes, mostly outward, some of it hurled back inside the car by the solid trunk. Steel crumples inward, trapping the girl's right foot, freezing the seat belt around the girl's arm, and shoving the front seat forward.

The car goes still. The driver tries to open the door, fails, and pounds at the window. When it breaks, pieces of glass fly across the roadway to the opposite shoulder. A grubby rag, which the driver found earlier in the door pocket and used to clear the windshield, now serves to wipe away sharp glass from the frame.

The driver climbs out, then uses the rag to wipe down everything that might have been touched (snagging a thread in a rough corner, caught on film by the police photographer the next day.) The door's handle, window surround, its inner side. The radio dial, rear-view mirror, and steering wheel. Stretch inside for the brake release and door pocket, though he misses—call him *he*, for the present—a few minor places along the back of the steering wheel. After all, it is dark inside the car. And he's in a hurry, since even on this road, he may not be alone for long.

The figure then stretches inside again to catch the sleeve of the girl in the passenger seat. He pulls. Bits of glass fall to the floor when she slumps onto the seat, and more when he wrestles to press the hand against the places he has just wiped: steering wheel, gear shift knob. But then it stops—he can't reach the door latch or brake release with her fingers. He half-lies across the window frame, but can't quite touch her other hand, to get it free from the damned belt.

He'd have to climb back inside, right on top of the girl.

Maybe he hears the sirens start up, through the cold night air. Maybe the farmer's flashlight catches his eye, or he hears the bark of a dog. Maybe he just decides that he's done enough, and no one will notice.

In any event, he does not try for any right-hand prints, just lets go of her arm and drops the rag, either on the ground or in the car, where it will fall out when Henry Belmonte, tonight's first responder from the DLPD, uses a crow bar to pry open the door, a very few minutes in the future.

And then he walks away. The sky is clear, the moon is giving enough light (*moon nearing first quarter*, says the note from Ray Schulman) to show the rickety gate and the stubbled grass beyond. When the sirens stop along Pipeline Road, he is two fields away.

∽

And the driver is right: no one notices the inconsistencies. Poor, troubled girl: went to a party, got a little high, borrowed a car, ended up against a tree. It would be kinder to her family if we called this an accident and quietly put away the film and the fingerprint cards, burned her bloodstained clothing, let her go to her Catholic grave. Nothing to see here, sadness is all.

No one notices, until three decades later the girl's sister happens to have a conversation with an inquisitive teenage daughter, and decides to ask a few questions, which lead to a few more, which lead to Ray Schulman and then to me, drinking coffee across a pitted table from Al Hawkin, looking into my former partner's steely gaze.

"If your sister grabbed the wheel, it doesn't matter a whole lot why she didn't want to be driven down that road. It could be anything from manslaughter to second degree murder—or even felony murder, depending on what the driver was doing at the time. But from where we sit, it doesn't matter."

It didn't matter, because any charges brought would be up to the DA. It was not up to Al or to me, as a sister or as a cop. But oh God, what had Patty got herself into, along that road?

Come on Kate, I ordered, *pull yourself together. Then was then, now is now. And you're a cop. Go with what you know.*

I pushed away the cup, straightened my shoulders. "Okay, Captain Cold Case. What do we do now?"

XIII

W hat we did now was make another list and divide that up. My first task was a long phone call with the Captain, explaining what had happened and asking permission to be, basically, seconded to the Cold Case unit. Normally, a cop wouldn't work the murder of a family member, but in this case, exceptions could be made—but only for one week, and only when it came to the background material.

"You get anywhere near identifying a suspect, it's hands off, right?" he said. "You do nothing, absolutely nothing, that would give a lawyer reason to get a case thrown out, you got me?"

"Absolutely."

"And this is not priority. If something else comes up, I need you back here. Otherwise, let me know how it goes. And Martinelli?"

"Sir?"

"Good hunting."

❧

"You're going down there *again?*"

"I know, that drive doesn't get any shorter."

"Kate, that's not what I mean. What is going on? Why are you packing a bag?"

"Because like I say, the drive to Diamond Lake doesn't get any shorter." I shoved in a sweatshirt and zipped the case shut, then turned to take Lee's hands. "Honey, I actually don't know what's going on. I hope I don't end up spending the night, but since it's a three-hour round trip at the best of times, I'm taking a few things just in case. We'll talk it over when I get back, and you and I can decide how much to tell Nora. But this is something I have to do."

"As a sister, or as a cop?"

"Both."

"Okay," she said—then stepped forward to wrap her arms around me. Which made me all the less eager to drive off, but I did.

Lisa Ferraro—Diamond Lake's Princess Di wannabe—had accumulated the faintest of digital footprints since the day she'd grinned at Patricia Martinelli over a painted backdrop. She'd married, had two kids, divorced, and vanished. No arrests, no headlines, no election to public office—at least, not under either surname I had for her.

I doubted she'd actually disappeared. As with many small towns, Diamond Lake's older records were slow to be scanned and uploaded to a database. I could spend hours online and on the phone, or I could go down there—yet again—and talk to people like the bakery owner, the librarian, Lisa's old teachers, and maybe even the chief of police.

So it wasn't the coffee that made me start at the Village Bakery—or not just the coffee. Being morning, the overhead customer bell was kept ringing, and the only empty seat was at a shared table under the window. The red-haired owner greeted me as a regular, but I carried my coffee and muffin over to the empty chair until there was a lull at the counter.

When the bell slowed, I took my phone up and showed her the yearbook pictures. "I'm looking for a woman who went to Diamond Lake High back in the eighties. Does this girl look at all familiar to you?"

I wasn't expecting much from the Bakery other than caffeine and calories, but the woman squinted at the little screen and said, "I think so. Can't remember her name, though."

"Lisa," I prompted.

"Ferraro—oh, sure! She was older than me, but she lived around here for a long time. Had two adorable little girls—twins, they were.

Lived north of town. She was married for a while to some sleazy guy. Real estate? Lawyer? Something, who dumped her for his… secretary?" She shook her head, and her eyes came back into focus. "Sorry, that's all I remember."

"No, that's great. But she's not still here?"

"If she is, I haven't seen her, not for years."

"What about any friends or relatives who might know where Lisa went?" Someone had come in, so when the baker's gaze went to the side, I moved rather than stand in the way of commerce. But instead, she brought the new customer into the discussion.

"Hey there, Susan—look, this lady's asking about Lisa Ferraro. Remember her? Tall, blond, twin girls, used to help out with the Diamond Lake Players productions?"

"Her married name was Mancini," I offered.

"There's a blast from the past," the Susan beside me remarked. "Didn't she move into some commune?"

"Really?" said my red-headed assistant sleuth.

"Not a hippie one, an artistic one. Somewhere in the Bay Area. Berkeley? Oakland—no, it was Santa Cruz." Santa Cruz wasn't exactly Bay Area, but I nodded. "And she changed her name. As a feminist thing, you know?"

I nearly said that no, I didn't know what a "feminist thing" might be, but I kept the encouraging look glued to my face. "Any idea to what?"

Her face scrunched up in thought. "A Greek goddess. Started with an A?"

Which was most of them. "Aphrodite? Artemis? Athena?"

"That's the one, Athena!"

"Lisa Athena?"

"I guess. Or maybe she just uses Athena."

Oh, these artistic types, I thought but did not say, and asked a few more questions. But that was all either of them knew, and other customers had come in, so I thanked them and retreated to the dregs of my coffee.

But this seemed to be my day, because a quick search for "Lisa Athena, artist" gave me a painter who lived in Santa Cruz. And when I called for images, up popped one of about the right age and height, with hair that might once have been blond.

If it was Lisa Ferraro, she'd sure left the Princess Diana look behind her.

~⚬~

Two hours later, after I'd met dead ends at Diamond Lake's high school, library, and police department, I sat in my car and returned to the search function on my phone. It took a while, hunting for "Lisa Athena" contact information, but I eventually came up with a gallery that sold her work. I phoned them, got a recording with a referral number, called that, got put on hold—and was finally speaking with a human being, a woman with a brisk manner and an accent from India.

"Good afternoon," I said. "I'm trying to reach one of your artists, named Lisa Athena, or just—"

"She goes by Athena. Just Athena."

"Fine, thanks. So, I know you probably—"

"We don't give out phone numbers."

"I know you probably don't give out contact information," I said more firmly, "but would it be possible for you to give her my number, and ask her to call me?"

"Is this about a sale?"

"It could be."

"Because this isn't a—"

My turn to cut her off. "You're not a message service, of course, but it's kind of important and I'd appreciate it if you'd try. You have a pencil? My name is Kate—er, Casey Martinelli. Athena knew my sister. Shall I give you the number?"

Unspoken questions crawled out of the phone, but after a minute, her grudging voice prompted me to give the number, and she wrote it down. When she hung up—after reiterating that she really couldn't promise anything and didn't expect Athena would come by soon anyway—I sat and studied the screen's phone display for a while.

I should go home.

I didn't.

XIV

A drive to Santa Cruz, unrepentant enclave of the Sixties, had also been a part of that very first homicide case of mine. So had artists, for that matter. The freeway exit dumped me in town and I followed my phone's instructions to a parking garage, walking down a street of shops, cafés, and homeless people to the gallery.

Athena's work was hanging toward the back, and was better than I'd anticipated. No Greek goddesses in sight, or even a trace of the Feminine Spirit, merely calm, competent depictions of local landscapes: redwoods, streams, and a stormy ocean.

"They're great, aren't they?" a voice asked.

Not, fortunately, the Indian woman I'd talked to on the phone.

"I like the one of kids playing in the river."

"That's the San Lorenzo, maybe five miles from here."

I made a point of stepping forward to look at the price, and nodded as if I were impressed with how reasonable it was. "It's really great. And in fact, I've been trying to reach the artist. I wonder if you'd be able just to give her a ring and see if she might be free to meet up? I don't have a number for her, and she's not in the book."

"Are you a friend, or something?"

"We fell out of touch, but I'd love to see her. If she's busy or doesn't want to see me, no problem, but she and my sister were really close, back in the day."

91

I was the only person in the shop, and after all, I had looked at the price tag on a $725 purchase without recoiling in horror. "We don't normally disturb our artists…"

"Totally understandable. And if she's busy, I'll just leave you a note to give her, next time she's in. Though it's a pity to miss the chance. Not sure when I'll be back."

I moved my attention to the next painting, larger and more expensive, and the woman went off to phone the artist known as Athena.

The artist answered the call. I listened to the gallery worker explain, but when she tried to hand me the phone, I gave her one of my cards instead—one without the SFPD logo—and let her read the number into the phone. I didn't really want my business to enter the town's shopkeeper gossip.

When she'd hung up, I thanked her, told her I'd think about that river painting, and walked out.

The phone rang before I hit the next street.

Ten minutes later, I was driving up into the hills.

And less than an hour after reaching town, I was shaking hands with the key to my sister's past.

My first impression was that I'd found the wrong person. My second was, *She chose the wrong myth.*

Her gray-blond hair was matted into long, finger-thick Medusa-dreads, studded here and there with varicolored beads. They must have weighed ten pounds when dry, and God knows how she managed to keep her balance when it was wet. With all that on top and a pair of purple-rimmed glasses beneath, it was hard to tell what she looked like. I had the impression of a tall, slim, tan woman a little younger than me, with a very strong grip.

"You're Patty's older sister—I remember you!"

"You've changed a bit since your yearbook photo," I replied.

She had a great laugh, as she stood back to welcome me in. "Is that how you found me? From the yearbook?"

"It was a roundabout process, but you know small towns, there's always someone who knows someone. Wow, what a great view."

Her rambling wooden house was perched on top of a hill with trees up close and a vineyard below. The vineyard, the view, and an offer of coffee took us past the first stages, and when we were settled at the table in the corner of her homey kitchen, I handed her my card—the real card, complete with gold star.

"You're a cop," she said.

I have heard all kinds of nuance to that simple phrase over the years. Alarm, mistrust, loathing, incredulity—but to my relief, her reaction was mild, little more than curiosity.

"I am, yes. Which would have amazed my sister."

"That was so sad, about her. The way she just… was gone. Patty was a fabulous person, fun and rude and full of life. It was tough, losing her. Well, I don't have to tell you that. But I should have said it at the funeral. I was so afraid I'd burst into tears, I didn't even say hi."

"You were there, at her funeral? I'm glad—though looking back, it's just a blur."

"I can imagine."

"I do remember a bunch of her friends there, mostly girls. But hey—I always wondered, I had the impression that Patty had a guy she was pretty serious about. Was he there, do you think?"

The way her eyes bounced away to intently study the window told me that I'd hit gold in the first five minutes. Not that she replied right away.

"Oh, I don't know, was there…? She didn't always tell me things, you know… Oh—I meant to put out some cookies."

She was a lousy liar, but I let her go off to the kitchen, then change the conversation when she got back.

But in the end, kids and art and Diamond Lake and how great Santa Cruz was ran dry. I gently brought her back to the point.

"Athena, I really do need to know about her boyfriend."

"Oh, honey, this was thirty years ago. What does it matter?"

I was not about to tell her why it mattered. On the other hand, I had to give her something that would pry it out of her. And unlike Athena, I am not a bad liar. I made an act out of hesitation, took a breath, and raised my eyes to hers. "Because I didn't ask, thirty years ago. Because I turned my back on Patty's death and let it go, and now

I find it's been festering away all this time—that I didn't care enough to ask. I have a daughter, just about her age. She's meeting boys, and she's getting stung.

"I'm fifty-two now. It's about time I asked myself whether or not Patty committed suicide because I wasn't there for her."

"I've never believed that Patty killed herself."

"But there was talk, right?"

"Small town, there's always talk."

"She died the end of January. I'd come home for Christmas, but we hadn't really been close for a year or two. However, you and she were, weren't you?" I was afraid she was going to ask how I knew, and force me to admit to a guess based on a yearbook grin. But she didn't ask.

"Yeah, we were close, for the first couple years. But at the end of our Junior year, she started hanging out with another crowd, and didn't have as much time for me."

"I'd heard that she was going around with—not a rough crowd, since this is Diamond Lake we're talking about, but maybe a little edgier."

"The rough crowd was where she came from. These were the rich kids."

"North-town?"

"That bunch, yes. I mean, I lived at the edges of north-town, but I'd never hung out with them. I thought they were playing games with her—you know, pick up the outsider and string her along until she makes a spectacular fool of herself."

"The viciousness of students," I commented.

"Laughing at her behind her back. Anyway, I let her know that I wasn't going to join her, so she drew back a little."

"There was a boy," I said. "Kid with dark hair and a leather jacket. Might've had tattoos."

She shook her head, dreads spilling all around. "I knew there was somebody, but all she'd do is drop hints."

"You remember any of those hints?"

"This was thirty years ago—how would I remember that?"

"You're pretty clear with the other things."

"Sorry," she said. "I know he was from north-town, so he'd have been good looking and had money. And she acted like he was older. But I'm pretty sure he was still in school, so that would've meant he was a Senior. Other than that, she kept it vague and teasy. Sort of Romeo and Juliet, you know? She'd have told me eventually, but…"

"Yeah. Well, that's a help anyway, and if you—"

"I also think he may have been some kind of outsider. Someone we hadn't grown up with, like most of the boys. Cause I remember thinking that had to be a big part of his appeal."

I laughed. "You're right about that, it's hard to find much mystery in a kid you went through elementary sch—"

I froze, as the piece slid into place. Outsider. North-town. A senior. No. *No!*

And yet…

XV

I don't actually remember thanking the dread-headed artist or leaving Santa Cruz. I'm not even sure how I got home, although I must have driven—and without hitting anything, since my undamaged car was out in front the next day.

The first thing I knew, Lee's voice broke the silence in my office. "Kate, it's three in the morning—what on earth are you printing at this hour?"

I pulled off my reading glasses and dropped them onto Officer Belmonte's notes, the ones made before the case was tidied away as an accident. He had comments on trapped feet and outstretched arms, and noted the odd position of the prints raised along the steering wheel. He'd kept records of where the swept-up glass had come from (in case they found that another car was involved—even in 1983, forensics could identify types of glass.) His evidence box also included the logbook he'd started, recording officers on the scene and the plates of passing cars. Or rather: the passing car.

After the initial flurry of activity around the accident site—when the paramedics had left and the on-call officer and first responder Henry Belmonte went back to their beds—the DLPD had left a patrolman at the scene. His job was to keep anyone from moving things around before the photographer returned by daylight. Having done that sort of job in my rookie years, I imagined that he'd been at least half asleep when the other car came down Pipeline Road.

The logbook recorded it as 4:12 AM. It came from the direction of the quarry. It was forced to stop, there being a patrol car across the road—and though the logbook didn't say, the officer would have parked on the town side of the accident.

Officer Columbo (whose name no doubt brought him grief, over the years) saw the approaching headlights and got out of the cruiser, walking across the broken window-glass to talk to the driver. Officer Columbo was in his first year on the force. Officer Columbo knew the kid who was driving, having been friends with his older brother all through childhood. And Officer Columbo knew that the kid's story—he'd fallen asleep out at the quarry, while waiting for some buddies to show up with beer—had the ring of truth, since he'd hung out at the quarry himself when he was that age, smoking and drinking beer.

And Officer Columbo nearly ended his career then and there, by letting his friend's brother drive across an active crime scene to go home.

That Columbo dutifully recorded the boy's name, license, and contact info would not have saved him from an almighty lecture from his Chief, and I imagined there was a reprimand buried in his file from that night.

The boy's name led me to an adult record, including prison time for involvement in a robbery—he having been hired to drive the non-getaway car. Failures behind the wheel had been a theme in his life, up to and including its end in a drunk-driving accident so spectacular, it might have ended up on the wall of Al's forensics guy.

His death had taken me a couple of hours to dig out, and left me at three a.m. with another dead end, a lot more questions, and a sense that I now knew what I was looking for, when it came to the shape of the puzzle's final piece.

I rubbed at my bleary eyes, and asked my wife a question. "Can I tell you a story? And ask you if it makes sense?"

"Sense to me as a person? Or as a psychotherapist?"

"Both, I guess. But mostly your professional take on it."

"All right. But I need a cup of tea."

"Coffee?" I suggested to her back, but when she returned, she was carrying two cups, and neither of them contained a trace of caffeine.

She settled into the room's comfortable chair and prepared to listen.

༄

The car is driving stupidly fast along Pipeline Road. The boy behind the wheel is preoccupied, aggressive, taunting his passenger on a wave of hormones and booze. In the past quarter hour, the girl in the passenger seat has gone from warm anticipation to cold terror—of him, of what the change in him means, of what lies at the end of the road.

He's talking crazy, and she wants out.

...Or maybe they had a fight and now he's simmering away in silence, this big, male person she thought she knew. The one she couldn't believe had picked her out for attention, who'd made jokes and admired her and made her feel good about herself. Whose parents were rich and so strict, he'd asked her to keep their relationship secret, just for a while...

Whether he's shouting or silent doesn't matter. What does matter is that she's afraid of him—more afraid of him, and of where he's taking her, than of what she's about to do.

He doesn't notice her left hand creeping down to where the latch emerges from the fold of the seat. Doesn't notice the faint click of its release, or the slow retraction of the strap across her body. The headlights, on high, show that break in the trees where the farmer's tractor goes, a gap that they'll be past in a few seconds—but which, if they steered into, would let the car smash through the flimsy gate and into the field beyond.

All she'd have to do then is get her door open and run. He'd come after her, sure, and yes, he was fast, but so was she and it would take him a while to get out and come around the car, and as soon as she got away from the headlights, he wouldn't see which way she'd gone, not if she was really quiet.

Anyway, he wouldn't hang around for long, would he? He'd be too worried about getting the car she'd borrowed for him back onto the road and away. He'd want to get home before morning, so his parents wouldn't notice he was gone.

So, a split second before the gap in the trees begins, she wraps her hand around the nylon strap and lunges forward to pull at the wheel.

But he's too fast, and too strong. He yanks the wheel back and hits the brakes. As the car begins to lose traction, his right arm swings out and the world explodes—twice. The first time is when his forearm smashes against her face, and she cries out. The second time, before she even feels the pain… the world ends.

For the driver, the noise of the crash is overwhelming, the force stunning. He half-lies against the strap of his seat belt for long seconds… then comes to, pulling himself upright on the wheel. He looks through the windshield, confused: one headlight is out. The other points crazily up into the branches over the road.

The road—that fucking bitch! God, he hurts! Gingerly, he reaches up to turn on the dome light, and there she is, leaning up against what used to be the window and is now a slab of tree bark. Is that what they hit? There's no expression on her face, her eyes staring at nothing. Is she dead?

He takes hold of her wrist. Nothing. Jesus, he's going to be in shit now. Stupid bitch, all her fault, worse than her—

Wait. His hand goes back to the light, plunging the car interior into darkness. Think. Nobody knows he's here—nobody who would talk. It wasn't *him* who borrowed the car. Maybe…

His vision creeps back, the headlight giving him the dim outlines of the car. Maybe it was all her fault—or maybe it was *only* her fault.

His fingerprints had to be all over—but what would this look like without them?

Almost without instruction from his brain, his left hand

reaches down for the rag he'd used earlier to clear the fog off the shitty windshield. Any place he'd touched: steering wheel, radio, brakes, gear shift, and seat-belt. Don't forget the dome light switch.

But now the fucking door won't open. In a panic, he bashes his fists against the window until it gives way, shooting glass out across the road.

He uses the rag to swipe the pieces out of the tracks, then climbs out, wincing at the strained muscles and aching shoulder, using the rag again to take the prints off the door and handles.

He can be gone before anyone comes along.

But studying the girl's hand, limp on the seat beside her, gives him an idea. These were small-town cops, sure, but what if they notice that somebody wiped off the fingerprints? Even Barney Miller might wonder about that.

He leans inside and reaches for her left wrist again—jumping as she seems to lean toward him. But it was only her body following her arm, so he holds her hand and presses her fingers against the wheel, the gear knob, anything he can reach.

The right hand is a problem—it's caught on something. He looks at her, lying face-down and bleeding all over the seat of her friend's car, and really doesn't like the idea of climbing inside to get her hand out of the belt. It felt creepy—and anyway, he'd get blood on his jeans. Like that wouldn't be suspicious.

And really, so what? So the little bitch only left fingerprints on part of the car. They'd never notice.

So he makes a last swipe with the rag around the door and tosses it away.

He'd never intended to kill the bitch, only to use her as payback. Two years ago, the little bitch's snob of a sister had freaked out and nearly killed him with that piece of pipe. All he'd planned to do was feel her up a little, have a laugh with the guys—but instead, she'd gone nuts and sent his whole fucking life down the drain.

A year and a half later—a year and a half of headaches and no sports and tanking grades—he'd noticed the younger sister and come up with an idea.

Well, he'd noticed the sister a while before, but every time he'd looked at her, it would make his head hurt.

He'd finally worked up his nerve.

…Or maybe, over Christmas, he happened to spot the older sister walking through town like she owned the place, and it pissed him off.

Either way, before the New Year, he'd made his play for the girl, and she fell right into his hand.

In two weeks, he was screwing her.

Ten days after that, he gave her some bullshit story about his car, so it would stay in his driveway tonight for the world to see. He told her to borrow a car from someone at the party she was going to, and pick him up at a quarter to twelve. They'd go for a moonlight drive down Pipeline Road. It'd be romantic.

Until she saw that his guys were there, too.

His friends had waited all night. They could see something had happened, what with the sirens and the lights. All but one of them decided to get out of there before the cops came looking, and set off home across the fields. But the kid whose car they had come in was more or less trapped there. It wasn't until four in the morning that he decided to try driving out, and met Officer Columbo.

Patty's killer also walked away, and got away. Twice now, these damned Martinelli females had nearly been the end of him. The thing was, he wasn't stupid. And he might be reckless, but he did feel fear. That night he was filled with rage and hormones and the anticipation of sweet revenge—but in the aftermath, he had enough self-control to look at the danger face-on, and learn from it.

What he learned was: Don't Go There. Take care with the temptations of revenge, when it means you're flirting with a charge of kidnaping and murder.

It was a lesson he took to heart. He was never again picked up by the police. He finished school, went on to college, used family money for a software startup that grew into mega-millions based largely on its CEO's looks, charm, and reputation for successful risk-taking. There were rumors about him, but what hugely successful businessman didn't carry a shadow?

Mark Fields had learned his lesson that night, driving too fast along Pipeline Road.

XVI

L ee's eyebrows rose at the name. "You don't mean…?"
"Yes. *The* Mark Fields." Software billionaire, man-about-town on the San Francisco Peninsula, owner of one of the biggest homes in the big-home territory of Woodside, Mr. Philanthropy when it came to Bay Area schools.

Meaning that Patty's Leather Jacket admirer in 1983, and my letterman-jacket assailant from 1981, had been one and the same.

"But why? What was that about ruining his life?"

"Ah. Yes. About that."

I gave her the condensed version of my history with the boy: would-be Lothario; dark alley; galvanized pipe. She had more of a reaction than Al had, though she found it easier to agree that, as a sixteen-year-old, he might have been after domination, rather than outright sex. What concerned her more was my willingness to let shame sweep away my childhood. It took a while to get her therapist mind off that and back to my proposed explanation.

"So, what do you think? Is that version of the accident possible? Yes," I said to hold off her automatic response, "you're going to say that anything human is possible, but what I want to know is, am I off in the high weeds here? Joining the tin-hat brigade?"

"What's his history? For example, does he have a police record from when he was young?"

"He does have a juvenile record, but it's closed, so I can't see what he was picked up for."

"And since then?"

"He's never been processed as an adult—in fact, he's not in AFIS at all, which means he's never served in the military, hasn't been arrested, and never had to go through a background check. Though that seems unlikely, for someone who runs a software company."

"How old was he at the time of the accident?"

"Not quite eighteen. And clean since then—though reading about him online, he seems to have a reputation for being in-your-face with people who piss him off. A bar fight. Two or three women claiming he shoved them around before they went silent."

"Let me guess: all of them bought off?"

"Like I say, rumors are. And he's a philanthropist, but he didn't start up his nonprofit until he was a billionaire several times over and people were commenting on how little he gave back. So he donates now, mostly to schools—and mostly places willing to stick his name up on a building."

"Married? Kids?"

"He's been married three times, has four kids, all of them stayed with their mothers after the divorces."

"I don't have to ask whether he takes physical risks, because even I have seen that picture of him hanging off Half Dome. And being a hugely successful entrepreneur, we can take it as given that he hits the 'deception' and 'self-centered' boxes on the sociopathy check-list."

"So that's a yes?"

"Is Mark Fields a sociopath? He could be—some degree of sociopathy is common enough among self-made kajillionaires. Could he have crossed the line into outright psychopathy? That's a diagnosis I couldn't begin to make without a detailed look at his history. Yes, a juvenile record is definitely a sign, since antisocial behavior manifests early, but in itself it doesn't mean anything. Does he have any close bonds, with family or friends? Has he shown any indications of real empathy or remorse, or are those superficial—apologies that open the door to some gain? How extreme is his risk-taking, and does he pull others along with him?"

A mental bell went off, and I reached for the heap of printouts I'd compiled. It took me a minute to find the page I was after.

"This was taken two years ago. He and some friends were at a ski resort where he'd booked the entire run for himself, and they triggered an avalanche. One of the friends was killed. This one is going to the hospital."

She studied the photograph. A crew of paramedics and mountain rescue personnel, a figure on a stretcher with neck brace and splinted leg—and beside him, one hand resting on the man's chest, Mark Fields.

Laughing.

Lee chewed her lip.

"I know," I said. "It could be what the caption says, relief at the rescue. But…"

"So you think he was driving the car when your sister died. And that he hid his involvement afterward. Panicky kid, running away from an accident—after thirty years, would anyone prosecute him for it?"

"Exactly what Al and I wondered. Technically, leaving the scene itself counts as a hit-and-run—a felony. He could be charged with involuntary manslaughter. But a rich kid with influential parents? I doubt Diamond Lake would've gone after him even at the time. And now? A good lawyer and a public apology read from a sheet of paper would make it disappear."

"There's a 'but' in your voice."

"There is. Because if he was in the process of committing a serious crime when she died, that's a whole different matter. That could make it felony murder."

"What kind of serious crime?"

"Felony drunk driving, say, or fleeing a robbery. Or kidnaping."

"That's why your scenario has him abducting her."

"It would explain some things. Al and I both think it's worth looking at."

"I take it you don't have any evidence? You'd have mentioned it."

"Nothing direct, you're right. What we do know is that he's bright. And though yes, even bright kids can panic, I'd have thought that a rich kid's automatic reaction would be, 'Oh crap, drunk driving—well, Mom and Dad will get me off.' And not being eighteen would have made things easier. Plus that, it's pretty clear Patty was already sleeping with him—which in the Eighties, especially considering how she tended to dress, would have made any rape accusation go away. So if their relationship was consensual, how could anyone accuse him of kidnaping?

"Unless there was something else—some reason to scare him into wiping his prints and getting as far away as he could. Such as, something he'd planned that would both punish me and restore him in the eyes of his buddies? Using the way he'd tried before, but had it go wrong on him."

"Conspiracy to assault."

"At this point, it's purely speculation. But we do know there was a boy that age who spent the night in his car, out at the end of Pipeline Road. And I personally can testify that Mark Fields had a history of leading his friends in an assault on a girl. When it comes to why he would be so eager to distance himself from the accident, an intention to set up my sister for a gang rape would explain it."

Lee studied the handsome, laughing face: perfect teeth, money in all directions, utter confidence. Then she looked up at me. My wife, the love of my life, who had paid the price of a bullet when my job followed me home—this woman looked across at me and said, "If that's the case, why has he left you alone for all these years?"

The room seemed to drop away from under me. My breath stopped—possibly my heart.

Good God. I'd been so focused, so wrapped up in finding a villain to my sister's story, that I hadn't paused to study the larger pattern.

I took a breath. "Aversion therapy, maybe?"

"I'm not joking, Kate."

"Sorry, I didn't mean… Look, if anything about our theory is correct, then the fact that I scrambled his brains had to've made a deep impression on—God, again, sorry. But wouldn't you say that even a predator can learn by aversion? He made two runs at the Martinellis, both of which went catastrophically wrong. Somewhere in his mind must be the feeling that he should steer clear of me. And anyway, Diamond Lake was small stuff to him. He's a multi-billion-aire now. Why would he even think about it?"

"Unless you remind him."

The long, long day washed over me. I sat back in the chair, closing my burning eyes. "You think I should drop it?" I asked after a while.

"I think you need to be really, *really* careful. And I think that, going forward, you need to stay well back from any prominent role. Make it look like something the machine kicked up, investigating an old case. Don't make it feel like you coming after him."

I nodded. "I'll talk to Al. See what we can do."

"Make sure Al understands the danger."

"But you think that story I told you does fit his profile?"

"Kate, you don't need me to tell you that."

No. I did not. After a while, Lee took my hand and we went to bed. I can't say I actually slept, in the few hours before the sun rose.

XVII

"Cold Case, Garcia speaking." Garcia was one of Al's colleagues, a young cop who'd lost part of a foot to a shooting.

"Hi Max, is Al in?"

"He said he'd be working from home for a couple of days. Try his cell?"

"I did, just thought I'd check there."

"Good luck," he said cheerfully, and hung up.

I closed down the phone and thumbed in a text to Al.

Need to talk.

But in the end, I couldn't wait. Instead, I crossed the hallway to stick my head in the captain's office. "You busy?"

"Never not, but I can give you a minute. What's up?"

"It's going to take more than a minute."

He gestured to the chair. I shut the door and sat down.

"I need to talk to you about a shit-storm I may be stirring up."

"This your cold case?"

"It's getting warmer."

He nodded; I talked. When his phone rang five minutes in, he shut it off. When his secretary tapped on the door ten minutes after that, he didn't even look up from my sheaf of printouts, just raised his voice to say that he'd be a while.

Half an hour after I'd shut the door, he gathered the pages, tapped them into order, closed the folder, and rubbed his face.

"Sorry," I said.

"No. I'm just thinking how to get at this. That box from Diamond Lake is in our evidence locker?"

"Everything but the film. And the only name connected to that is mine."

"And as far as you know, Diamond Lake never processed the rest of the evidence?"

"As I understand it, the officer in charge back in 1983—Belmonte—lifted a bunch of prints and was going through them, but once the department told him to call it an accident, he put the rest away without analysis."

"Then that's the first step."

"Okay, but Fields' prints aren't on any database I can get at."

"Have you two talked with Diamond Lake yet about jurisdiction?"

"Not yet."

"So there's nothing on record so far."

"There wasn't when I last talked with Al, which was yesterday."

"Then let's keep things under wraps. You hand-deliver the print cards to the lab, and tell whoever takes them that if a match comes up, I don't want it in the system. They can give it to you, me, or Al, period."

"They're going to think it's to do with Homeland Security."

"Let them think it."

"Yes, sir."

"Any other evidence waiting around? I suppose the car itself is long gone."

"Yes."

"DNA?"

"Belmonte sent her underwear off to be tested a few years ago, but there wasn't anything. Basically, all the box had was photographs, the print cards, a handful of broken window-glass, and a bag of stuff that looked like they'd swept it off the floor of the car. There's a few cigarette butts we could try, but I can't vouch for where the box was kept all these years." It didn't take much heat to degrade the DNA in saliva.

"Okay, put those in as well, with the same no-name order."

"Thank you, Captain."

"And if nothing comes back—if there's no evidence to tie your sister's death in to Mark Fields—then we drop it. Yes?"

"Absolutely."

∾

To be honest, I couldn't have said which I wanted: to find someone responsible for the loss of my sister, and risk waking up demons from the past, or to put it down as an unsolved cold case and keep my family in the dark.

Both Lee and the Captain were right. We had to pick our way through this potential mine-field, and not set a foot down until we were sure of our ground.

When Al finally phoned, I asked him where on earth he'd been.

"At my new club."

"You have a club?"

"Working out, you know?"

"Um, good for you."

"What's up?"

I told him about my conversation with the Captain. He listened, grunting occasionally, when I described what the Captain had said about secrecy.

"You taking the stuff to the lab today?"

"I thought I would. Why?"

"You know your sister's letter and that Polaroid you told me about? The one with the boy's ass? I think you should put those into evidence as well."

"What, you think we'll need it for a lineup?" I had to laugh at the idea of putting together an ID line of tattooed asses.

"Would be one for the records," he agreed mildly.

"Okay, I'll do it today."

But as I hung up, I wondered about that club. My partner had never been one for fitness, and yet the other day he'd eaten a salad, and now he was working out. Sure, we were all getting older, but— was there something he and Jani weren't telling us?

XVIII

The fingerprint results came back fairly rapidly—such as they were. Conveniently, Belmonte had gone so far as to assemble print cards that would eliminate the car's actual owner, Tony Cardone, and Patty herself. Most of the latents belonged to Cardone. Patty's, as I'd known early on, were exclusively from her left hand, and almost all in areas that were remarkably clean of other prints.

That left half a dozen unmatched prints from the car's driver side. Two of those the lab had identified as a man who ran a Diamond Lake garage back in the seventies and eighties, who had died of natural causes in 2001. Another print was from the car's previous owner, who had sold the car when he went into the Army. Three prints were not in the system: a partial from the gear shift that was probably too small to use; one from the brake release, fairly clear and nearly complete; and a partial that was clear but small, from the window crank handle.

I phoned Al, and yet again was shunted to voice mail. This time he called back in just a few minutes, from some place with a lot of background noise.

"What's up?" he asked.

"I got the results of—Al? Can you hear me?" Loud male voices tumbled out of the phone, drowning out anything he might be saying.

"Hold on." The voices faded, cut off. "You still there?"

"Where are you?"

"My club."

"Again? Al, what on earth—"

"Busy here, Kate, what do you need?"

"I—Al, never mind, give me a ring when you have a few minutes to spare."

The phone went dead. I pulled it away from my ear and stared at its number pad. What the hell was the man up to?

But instead of phoning, twenty minutes later, he sent a text—an address down in Palo Alto, with the words:

Come get me.

Before I could text back to say that a trip down the peninsula wasn't really convenient, a second message arrived.

Now.

Pls.

So I sent back:

Be at least 45 minutes.

And received:

Fine.

What could I do except get in the car and drive down to Palo Alto?

The address was a coffee house. Al came out before I could park, a paper bag in one hand, a to-go coffee in the other, and an old sports bag slung over his shoulder.

He rested the coffee on the roof while he opened the back door, dropping the gym bag on the floor but placing the paper sack with care on the seat. He retrieved the coffee and got in front, handing me the cup. It was almost warm.

"I guess that isn't a pastry for me?" I asked, pointedly glancing at the backseat.

"Oh, it's for you, but it's not a pastry. I brought you a water bottle. An empty one. Complete with both saliva and fingerprints."

I stared at him. His blue eyes were beaming with pleasure.

"You got Mark Fields' water bottle?"

He ducked his head to look through the windshield, nodding across the street at a sleek building with a lot of sleek people going through its doors. A building that housed a sports club so exclusive, the sign could barely be read from the street.

"Let me guess: your new club."

"Which has some interesting members." He dug into a pocket for his phone, unlocked it, and handed it to me.

It took a moment to make sense of the image: a wall covered by wooden doors with padlocks—an upscale locker room. With people—the figure on the right, blurred with motion, was fully dressed, but the other person, the man holding the towel...

I expanded the image, and grinned at the male buttocks, slightly pixilated but clearly emblazoned with the Gothic words KISS and MY, on either side of the crack.

"Al, you're a damn genius."

XIX

At a certain point in any case, investigators begin to weigh their bits and pieces of evidence, trying to decide if there's enough to justify a warrant, and eventually an arrest. A good defense lawyer—and the one on this case was sure to be the best—would argue every step of the way. The discarded bottle, the circumstantial evidence, the personal involvement of one of the investigating officers, on and on.

Say there was something in the evidence box that pointed at Fields. The thing had knocked around a rural police station for thirty years. Anyone could have put it there. And that faded Polaroid of a tattoo that bore a resemblance to one worn by Mark Fields? Who was to say that half the boys in his high school hadn't lined up for that same tattoo? Indeed, was there any reason to think Mr. Fields even knew Patricia Martinelli beyond passing her in the halls of the high school?

Your honor, we move to dismiss.

But it's not a cop's job to try the case. A cop's job is to put together enough evidence to make a prosecutor happy. For that decision, we needed to go back to our Captain.

This time, I let Al do the talking. And in the end, the Captain agreed that we did not have to put the case entirely on hold until the DNA report came back from the water bottle and the stuff from the car.

Which meant that Monday, Al and I were driving back to the Diamond Lake Police Department, for the all-important discussion about jurisdiction. This was one trip when Al didn't fall asleep. Instead, he stared out the window and made the occasional note. As we left the freeway, he spoke for the first time in miles.

"I think you should let me do the talking."

"Why? Because you and the Chief bonded over football?"

"It was baseball. And no, it's because you're too involved."

He had a point. And if anyone could establish a rapport, personal and professional, with Dan Ruckart, it was Al. "Okay. But don't forget to play the budget card."

"Small towns, tight budgets, got it."

A case could be tricky when different jurisdictions were involved. My sister had died in Diamond Lake: the SFPD had no authority here. However, if the investigation went where we thought it might, even if the town asked for FBI assistance, the trial itself would burn through a load of money. And considering that our suspect had a bigger income than the annual budget of Diamond Lake, even a young, eager-beaver DA would think twice about filing against him.

Chief Dan Ruckart was the first person we needed to convince. He looked a little pale by the time we finished. He glanced over to make sure the office door was shut—about the tenth time he'd done so—and rubbed his jaw, then reached out to shift the photographs around on the desk.

I thought he was going to turn us down.

"Mark Fields? Jesus."

"Believe me," Al said, "we know what we're asking."

"I don't think you do. He's given this town millions. The mayor's been in talks with the Fields Foundation about a new—ah, shit."

"Well, it was just a thought. We'll leave you out of it."

It being our proposed next step, namely, talking with any Diamond Lake High graduates who might remember a link between Patty and the Fields boy. Al and I, as outsiders, would have to set these up as formal interviews, while Chief Dan could slip questions into casual small-talk about the town's financial benefactor.

"No, I'll do it. And I better start now, before the mayor makes his announcement."

We stood. Al stuck out his hand. "You have the thanks of the San Francisco Police Department. And the apologies of two of its investigators, for having dumped this on you."

I finished gathering the folders and shook Ruckart's hand, too. "Thank you, Dan."

"If my department missed things back then, it'll be me who's sorry. Maybe Diamond Lake needs a Cold Case unit of its own."

Dan Ruckart was as good as his word. Two nights later, my cell phone rang at 8:30. When I answered, he spoke without a greeting.

"Three of your sister's friends knew she was going out with Mark Fields that January."

"Thank you."

"One of them would testify to that, the other two aren't so eager. You'll want signed statements, I'd guess."

"I think so."

"But you don't want me to talk to his buddies yet?"

"I think we need to wait until the next round of lab results come in. I'd rather have the DA make that call."

"Okay, I'll go back to the three women tomorrow, see how much I can get. And I'll have to schedule a talk with the mayor, warn him what's coming. And after him, the DA."

"You think he'll want to keep the case?"

"Not when the mayor points out it'll bankrupt the town."

"I am really sorry, Dan."

"Don't be. I liked this job, but it is what it is. 'Night."

Sleep well, I said to the dead phone.

One, and potentially three pieces to add to the picture we were building.

The next piece came two days later, with a late-afternoon phone call from the lab.

"You wanted me to test that rag and the cigarette butts, and compare them to the water bottle."

"Tell me they match," I pleaded.

"No blood on the rag, and I couldn't get anything off the cigarettes."

"Well, we tr—"

"But there was a piece of window glass with blood on it, and the DNA was still good."

"*And?*"

"They're a match. With your nameless boy suspect."

"Holy shit. Oh, Jesse, I owe your lab a Christmas party."

"Who's your suspect, anyway? I mean, all hush-hush, no names, it's why we worked it so fast. Must be a terrorist cell or something, right?"

"Or something."

"Ah, come on, Kate, you can tell me. We're good with secrets here."

"I'll see if I can let you know before it goes public, okay? That's the best I can do. But Jesse, again, thank you."

One tiny spot of blood on a crumb of safety glass. Two partial fingerprints in another kid's car. A tattoo, some thirty year-old memories, and an out-of-focus yearbook photograph...

Circumstantial threads, with no direct evidence in the lot.

Once we had a charge, subpoenas would fly. Interviews and interrogations; a warrant to search the Fields home, pointless as that would be after all these years. Talking to friends of the dead boy whose car had been logged by Officer Columbo, that night on Pipeline Road: did they know Mark Fields, back in the day? Medical records—had the hospital treated a banged-up kid that night? Did a local doctor have a walk-in patient?

Threads, all of them. But hell: threads were what captured the giant Gulliver. Why couldn't we financial Lilliputians capture the massively wealthy Mark Fields with ours?

I talked to Al, a conversation that looped back, again and again. Was there anything else we might do before taking things to the DA? What would he make of the evidence as it was? Would it be enough?

Mark Fields on the one side, threads on the other.

"I wish we had something else," I said.

"You want to wait?"

"I don't think we can. Once Chief Ruckart talks to his mayor, things will get out."

"We might get lucky. Might stay under wraps for a few days."

We tried to reassure each other that every case felt the same way at some point, but when we hung up, neither of us was fully convinced.

I dropped my head back, kneading at my stiff shoulders. Thed Bear watched me from the shelf, slumped against the books. "You can hang a man with a rope made out of threads, right, Thed?" I asked him. Not that we hang people anymore.

He merely contemplated the scarlet toenails on his right foot. Thed looked a bit strangled himself, I thought, with all those necklaces around his throat. I stood, stretched, and took him down, running my fingers through the cheap decorative pendants. The one on the top was a gaudy piece of Indian enamel-ware in the shape of a heart, a little locket nearly buried among the shiny unicorns and Berkeley hippie-beads that hid the long-buried silk neck-tie I had given him.

A heart-shaped locket. The last thing Patty had given him.

I lay Thed under the desk light. The heart was little more than a half-inch across, but it did indeed have a small indentation on the side. Smiling, I absently worked a thumbnail into it, pried—

And stared down at the tight little curl of hair that tumbled out.

Black hair.

My hands found a pair of heavy scissors in the drawer and cut right through the flimsy chain. The open heart dropped onto the top page of printouts. I moved Thed to the side and went back to the drawer for the magnifying glass, a joke gift from Nora. A lock of cut hair didn't provide much genetic material—but maybe Patty's boyfriend had objected to having a chunk of hair cut away. Maybe she'd had to retrieve her memento from his comb instead.

I stared through the magnifying glass, trying to see if there were any bulb ends, but I couldn't tell, not without pulling the curl apart. Taking care not to move too fast or breathe too vigorously, I folded the sheet around the little heart and its contents, and wrapped the thing with tape. A lot of tape.

They were only threads, hair-thin and fragile.

And yet…

XX

The hair in Patty's locket did contain DNA. It matched that of the blood on the broken window-glass. It also matched the saliva on the bottle from the fitness club.

Two of Patty's three friends gave Dan Ruckart written statements saying that the boy Patty had not-so-secretly been going out with that last month was someone who had later become really, really famous.

Ruckart also found one of Mark Fields' high school friends, who agreed to give testimony in exchange for immunity: he and three others had driven out to the old quarry that night, to drink beer and smoke dope while they'd waited for Mark—who had promised them a party. A party involving a girl. They'd heard the sirens, seen the lights, and three of them had abandoned the car and its driver to walk home across the fields.

Records from the Fields family doctor, long retired but slow to clear out his storage locker, revealed that Mark had been treated for a badly bruised left shoulder and a number of scratches on his hands, sustained when he "fell off his bike." The treatment happened the morning after Patty died.

And finally, forensic examination of an old leather jacket found in the Fields house in Diamond Lake—packed away with such memorabilia as Mark's letterman jacket and the running cleats he'd won his JV title in—revealed a smear of blood embedded in its right fore-arm, just where you'd expect from a back-handed blow to a passenger. The stain had been cleaned, and was too degraded for a DNA sample.

In the end, based on the Conspiracy to Rape admission from his one-time buddy, Mark Fields—*the* Mark Fields—was charged with felony murder. He was arrested, and would be tried, in San Francisco.

~

It was the top story on every Bay Area news channel, and aired before the first commercial break in the national news. Company stock prices sagged, spokesmen read cautiously worded protests, Fields stepped down as CEO of Fields Enterprises. There was talk of changing the company's name.

Word of the ass tattoo leaked—of course it did—followed rapidly by either the image itself or a Photoshopped recreation. The Fields ass became a well-known internet meme.

Diamond Lake is no longer in the running for a major Fields Foundation grant—in fact, the Foundation itself is far from a sure thing. But Dan Ruckart is still chief of police. And last week, I had a letter from Diamond Lake High asking if I would mind their setting up a small college art scholarship in the name of Patricia Martinelli.

The Fields trial itself won't begin for months, possibly years. Will he be convicted? Anyone who has seen a rich man's lawyers at work will doubt it. But will he recover?

I don't think so.

So far, Al and the Captain have managed to keep my name out of everything. I pray that my sister's killer never learns what I had to do with getting the investigation under way. It will be bad enough when he finds I'm providing evidence against him.

The night before the Fields arrest, I finally had my long-delayed conversation with Nora. As my carefully edited explanation went on, she picked up Thed to run her hands along his fur, as if reaching to him for comfort. I told her about Patty's relationship with a boy, a boy she thought she could trust. I described what Al and I had fitted together about my sister's bravery, her determination to save herself, when she discovered her boyfriend's true nature. About how I'd gotten a lot wrong, and some things right, all these years. And I gave her the barest outlines of the case against Mark Fields, stressing that this was something she couldn't talk about, outside her family.

"But you think he killed her."

"Indirectly, but yes, without a doubt he killed her."

"*The* Mark Fields."

"Nora, you do understand that you can't tell anyone what I've told you? I am trusting you with my job, here. If anyone finds out I've given you evidence in a case, I could be fired. And Fields himself could use it to get free."

I could see the last threat hit home. Her head, which had been bent over the bear while she listened, now came up, her eyes flaring with anger. "I won't, Mom. I'll never talk about it, ever. I promise."

"I know you won't, honey. I just needed to be sure you understood the consequences. Now, what do you think—did Mama Lee leave us any of that caramel ice cream you love?"

～

A newborn's wail, a doctor's news, the squeal of brakes. A car driving too fast on a lonely road.

My life as a cop started with a story I told myself, to try and make sense of my kid sister's death. When I had it, when I'd built a picture that explained the facts, I turned away from her and from my early years, to get on with life—until my daughter forced me to go back to my beginnings for a closer look.

These days, Thed Bear sits on a shelf in the living room, minus his heart locket. That is waiting with the other evidence, to do its part in the trial. I framed two pictures of Patty and added them to our family photo wall. Nora mentions her occasionally, like an aunt she once knew who moved far away.

The note under my dormitory room door had said: *Kate, your family's trying to reach you.*

And I think it has.

NOTES

Same-sex marriage was not definitively ruled on by the US Supreme Court until June, 2015. Kate and Lee were first married during the brief 2004 period when licenses were issued in San Francisco. In the eleven years that followed, some couples had to marry several times, until the law finally caught up with society.

∼

With thanks to retired SFPD Homicide Inspector Karen Lynch, Robert Difley, Master of Images, Sylvie-Marie Drescher, Bookshop Santa Cruz Publishing Coordinator, and my team of backup editors—Alice, Erin, Merrily, Lynn, and Zoë.

All these people have proved unfailingly generous with their time, scrupulously attentive to detail, and invariably patient with my mistakes.

And because writers by our nature both lie for a living and ignore sensible advice, none of these good folk should be held responsible for my own creative manipulations of grammar, geography, or the workings of the SFPD.

Laurie R. King
Santa Cruz, California